THE

MISER'S FATE.

𝕬 𝕽𝖔𝖒𝖆𝖓𝖈𝖊.

LONDON:

PUBLISHED BY G. PURKESS, COMPTON-STREET, SOHO; LLOYD, SALISBURY
SQUARE, AND SOLD BY ALL BOOKSELLERS

THE MISER'S FATE.

CHAPTER I.

SOME ACCOUNT OF THE NORBERRY FAMILY.—WHO AND WHAT THE GRANDFATHER
OF BOB WAS.—DUBLIN SIXTY YEARS AGO.

ABOUT seventeen years before the act of legislative union between Great
Britain and Ireland had passed, and when the west end of Dublin was the
seat of commerce, wealth, and industry, there resided in an antiquated mansion in the neighbourhood of James's-street, the remains of which are still
standing, a wealthy old miser named Nipper Norberry, of very retired and
eccentric habits. His residence was one of those tile-covered pent-house dwell-
ings, which formed the general class of private buildings in that city, something above two centuries ago; and he was more attached to it for the sake of
old associations, than any comfort or accommodation it afforded. His fathe

No. 1.

before him had made a fortune in the place, which he, like a wise and prudent son, had considerably increased ; and having no fancy for princely mansions in one of the squares (in truth there were few of them built at that time), he continued to reside there, enjoying more satisfaction in the accumulation of wealth than others find in spending it. The Liberties of Dublin, which are now a mass of ruins and dilapidated houses, inhabited by squalid, half-famished looking mortals, who would seem to be denied a resting-place in any other spot under Heaven, were at that time inhabited by merchants and citizens of good estate. There the hum of industry was heard on all sides, and although machinery was not brought to any great degree of perfection, still every hand was employed, and the fabric produced was at least as durable and of more intrinsic value than anything similiar in modern times. The fly-shuttle and the hand-loom were at work in the lower apartments of almost every building, and the silk throwsters and spinners were employed in the upper stories. Every dwelling was a little manufactory, where the artisan worked in his own abode, assisted and cheered on by the presence of a happy wife and family : he was then more moral and more healthy than the inmates of the great English factories of the present day, and his condition in life was infinitely superior. High-street, Thomas-street, Francis-street, James's-street, and all that part of the city west of Dublin Castle, was then a busy scene of active industry ; and here did the ancestors of many noble houses and peers of the present day amass that wealth, as successful traders, which purchased honours and titles for their posterity.

Amongst those quiet and prosperous citizens then occupying this district, lived our wealthy merchant, in the same house which had been occupied by his ancestors for some generations previously. If any one asked where Mr. Norberry lived, his next door neighbour, except he happened to be long resident in the place, could not tell, as he was generally designated "Old Hawk." After having retired from the more active pursuits of mercantile life, he took to lending money and discounting bills, which was then a very profitable trade, as the present legal facilities for the payment of debts did not exist, and bankruptcies and failures in trade were of very rare occurrence. In this occupation, still adding to his wealth, he remained unmarried for many years, his household consisting all the time of an old woman named Shue Shaugness, or, as she would say herself when speaking of her own respectability and her family connections in the county of Limerick, "Judith O'Shaugnessey ;" a servant man called blind Tim ; and a kind of clerk, who went backward and forward to the banks of Sir George Cold-brooke and Company, in Mary's Abbey, and Dawson and Coates, in Thomas-street, where his employer made lodgments and did other business in the banking line. Blind Tim lived on board wages, and slept in a stable loft which was attached to a warehouse on the other side of the street ; and old Shue was allowed nine-pence a week to get her dinner, and had the privilege of the master's tea-pot, with a round of the loaf every morning when he had breakfasted. He dined every day at a tavern, and paid in proportion to the quality of the viands consumed. The clerk had a small salary, and lodged in the house of a comb-maker opposite, where he was always within call or under his master's eye. Blind Tim's business was to take care of a pair of horses, each as old as himself, and to drive his master through the city in an old chaise which he had taken from a coachmaker in payment of a bad debt. There are many citizens still living who remember the equipage of Old Hawk, amongst whom might be mentioned a venerable alderman, who was then a handsome young lad, and in some way connected with the Norberry family, although Old Hawk held him in the greatest contempt as a coxcomb that would never rise in the world ; but his predictions in this respect were falsified. The horses were originally black, but had grown grey from age : the solitary occupant of the old coach was in perfect keeping with the driver and horses, and on the whole it might be said that a more suitably appointed "turn out" had been seldom seen in the fair city of Dublin. The tradesmen at work in the Liberty, and the very children in the streets, knew the rumble of Old Hawk's shandredan, as he drove about collecting his interest money, and the rents of various houses in that quarter of the town, of which he was the owner. Such is a short outline of the household arrangements and manner of living of Old Hawk until he was nearly sixty years of age, when he took it into his head to marry.

The social philosophy contained in the aphorism, "Tell me what sort a man's wife is, and I will tell you the life he led," has more wisdom in it than can be at once comprehended ; and it is a remarkable fact, capable of proof amongst us in every-day life, that misers, money-hunters, and men of lax morals, whether in high or low society, hardly ever form respectable matrimonial alliances. Whilst young, the sordid and avaricious will not wed with women of equal rank and fortune, the love of money still prompting them to enter upon fresh speculations which ends in disappointment. The man who is not guided by strict morality cannot appreciate female virtue or the endearments of the congugal condition ; and hence both are found either in the ranks of old bachelors, or they make matches in after life which seem to be a penalty upon the faults of their early days. An old bachelor is, notwithstanding, sagacious enough to know that any young woman of equal rank who marries him, does so for the purpose of spending his money, or in the hope of being shortly honoured by the appellation of "the rich window." The miser knows, too, a marriage of this description would considerably increase his expenses, and hence it is, that the matrimonial alliances of such men are made with women who are content to act in the double capacity of servant and wife.

Old Hawk, when nearly sixty, began to entertain serious notions of matrimony, and circumstances occurred which hurried him to the fulfilment of his intentions. One day that he had been more than usually successful in his money speculations, he dined according to the custom at his tavern, but having staid out late blind Tim went to bring him home. He had drunk rather freely, and when Tim arrived at the "Ram" in Augier-street, he found the landlord on the point of sending a messenger to Allen's livery stables and carriage yard in Lazor's-hill for a charriot to convey Old Hawk to his residence in James's-street, he being supposed unable to keep his perpendicular, even by the assistance of the watchmen, who, in the good old times, before teetotalism was thought of, were in the habit of conveying drunken people from one station to another, until arrived at their own home. This by the way, was often a very lucrative employment to those trusty guardians of the night, who generally eased the pockets of their protegees of any loose money or watches with which they might be encumbered. To tell the truth of Old Hawk, he had never before been qualified to receive the protection of the Dublin watchmen, who were constantly in the habit of visiting his tavern, as well as others, at a late hour of the night, to know if there were any drunken gentleman to be brought home, to whom they were always ready and willing to act as guardians and conductors.

On the night in question, two of those professional gentlemen had made a tour of inspection through all the sitting-rooms at the "Ram," with the view of ascertaining who would require their services, when, to their infinite joy, they discovered Old Hawk, amongst others, a fit subject upon which to exercise their philanthropic intentions. A golden world opened before them ; he was rich beyond bounds ; it was a long journey from the "Ram" in Aungier-street to his residence in James's-street, and all the gentlemen along the whole line, amongst whom the most perfect sympathy of sentiment and unity of purpose existed, would have at least paid themselves well for their trouble in conveying him home. The two officious worthies who thus offered thir services, told Tom Fogarty, the landlord of the "Ram" to give the old gentleman another go, and he would be just fit to travel ; they thought he was not sober enough to walk home himself, nor drunk enough to be quiet, so that unless he got a little more they apprehended they would have considerable trouble with him. Fogarty was an honest Munster man, who had made a little money by his calling, and had the reputation of treating his customers fairly and dealing honestly with the world ; he refused to allow the watchmen to interfere at all, and had proposed, as already stated, to send to Allen's for a chariot to convey Old Hawk and himself to James's-street, for he intended leaving him safe and sound under his own roof.   The professional gentlemen were deeply chagrined at this unexpected interference in a matter so much connected with their own interests, and they told Fogarty he might mark the consequences of his imprudence ; he ought to know the influence they had with Recorder Brad-street and all the magistrates; they never reported his house, although that might often have been done ; but if he did not allow them to mind their own affairs, they would open a new leaf, and send the bogtrotter back to Munster amongst the rebels, instead of allowing him to make money like a gentleman in the loyal city of Dublin.   Fogarty was inexorable to their threats and entreaties, and the messenger was going off for the chariot when blind Tim arrived, and the guardians of the night were obliged to depart, disappointed in their expectations, and vowing vengeance on the honest tavern-keeper.   In the mean time he who formed the subject of their discussion had sufficiently recovered from the effects of the brandy punch which he had taken, to understand the nature of the conversation, and to appreciate the honest intentions of his worthy host ; then the arrival of his faithful servant, who for upwards of thirty years had never seen him affected by intoxicating drink, seemed to act upon him like a galvanic battery, and he started from his seat with a vigour which astonished all the spectators.

"I have heard," said Old Hawk, "all that passed whilst those robbers, who are a disgrace to our city, were endeavouring to get me into their clutches, and I shall no longer hesitate in the prosecution of a purpose which has long occupied my mind, but which I have never yet had the resolution to avow ; you (looking at Fogarty) shall hear very soon what it is I have in contemplation ; there is perhaps no other man in existence who can so materially assist in the accomplishment of my project, and I am sure you will the more readily lend your aid when you find that what I intend to do will be of advantage to yourself ; but there is one barrier which must of course be removed before any thing can be finally accomplished.

Fogarty replied, that there was nothing in his power that he would not do to make Mr. Norberry happy, for he had been greatly honoured by the patronage which he bestowed on his house so long, as well as for the many friends whom he had recommended there.

Whilst this conversation was going on, the chariot which was to take Old Hawk home arrived at the door of the " Ram" and blind Tim proposed conveying his master thither without any further delay ; but his proposal was interrupted by an inquiry from the latter of—

"What is the hour?"

The landlord replied—

"Five minutes after twelve."

"Right !" said Old Hawk, "it was not twelve when the chariot was or-dered at Allen's, and I will therefore only have to pay ' day fare' for it."

It may be here stated, that in these good old times the price of a chariot for an hour, if engaged before twelve o'clock at night, was only a shilling, but between that and six o'clock in the morning the fare was one and sixpence, and the worthy old gentleman was anxious that he should have the benefit of an engagement made one minute before that hour, being thereby enabled to save sixpence.   The charioteer interfered by saying he admitted it was a minute or two before twelve when the order came, but the clock had struck before he had turned out, and he was therefore entitled to night fare.   A rejoinder from Old Hawk followed, by a recommendation from the landlord to compromise the matter, as it seemed to involve a point of law, and after some controversy it was agreed that the contending parties should split the difference between them, and leave the sum to be paid one and three pence, instead of one and sixpence.   Tim and his master entered the chariot, and on their arrival at home, he seemed to have become perfectly sober.

They discharged their charioteer, and entered their cheerless dwelling, which gave no sign of life, except the chirping of a swarm of crickets, that occupied the ground floor when all other company were absent. Old Shue had gone to bed, the fire was out, and blind Tim was obliged to go to a neighbouring watch-house to light a candle. On his return, Old Hawk took him into the parlour, which served the treble purpose of office, bed-room, and sitting room ; near the window was a strong oak desk with an iron railing round it, opposite which was a safe built into the wall ; at the other [end was a cupboard or press which served to hold the scanty viands and table-ware with which the house was supplied ;behind the door was a huge clock in an oaken case as large as a sentry-box, which had stood there for a couple of generations, and whose loud and healthy stroke gave promise that it would continue to vibrate long after many a human heart, bent on worldly gain, and fraught with plans calculated to oppress or deceive their fellow-men, had mouldered into dust. In another part of the room was a press-bed, which turned up into a niche in the wall ; there were a few oak chairs and two small tables of the same material, which completed the entire furniture of Old Hawk's state apartment.

When Tim entered with the candle, his master sent him in search of old Shue's firewood, and, after lighting a fire, he sat down, and they drew their chairs together. There are moments when the man who makes himself the outcast of society by his inordinate thirst for gold, and the sordid practices which he adopts in pursuit of it, feels that he is alone in the world, and that amongst the sons of men there is hardly one with whom he can reciprocate one kindly feeling, or in whom he can confide, either in the hour of success or of sorrow ; and that if there be one such friend, it is an old and faithful servant, who has entered into the feelings of his master, and becomes reconciled to his habits and his eccentricities. Tim was one of those faithful domestics, whose nature it was to be attached to any person or thing with which he was connected, and was, in point of fact, as fond of the old horses as he was of his master, and any esteem he might have to spare for a third object was given to old Shue. He was paid his board wages to the hour, and his standing wages were put to interest, which was paid quarterly and added to the principal, so that by careful management, under the direction of his master, he had amassed some money. The master was, besides, naturally quiet in his disposition, and never found fault with anything, provided he was successful in his money-getting pursuits, which was most generally the case ; so that Tim's situation was after all as agreeable as that of a man serving a titled master with a splendid equipage and a numerous retinue of servants. There was therefore a reciprocity of feeling between them, that alas ! seldom exists between master and servant.

"Tim," said Old Hawk, as the billets of wood that had been lighted blazed up briskly, "hand me the bottle of wine that is in the safe ; I was made a present of a dozen by Mr. Jolly, for whom I cashed a small bill ; we will take a glass before we go to rest : I want to tell you something of my great success to-day, and of my future intentions and prospects."

Tim complied, and, having uncorked the bottle, sat down opposite his master the wood fire burned cheerfully in the rusty grate, and gave an appearance of comfort to the apartment which it had rarely worn.

"Tim," continued Old Hawk, "put out that candle, the fire blazes so prettily that I think the candle light only spoils the effect of it ; and besides, conversation is pleasanter by a cheerful fire than if the room was completely illuminated."

"Why," said Tim, "that's just what I was thinking, and I was really going to put it out before you spoke."

"Ah," replied the master, "you are just what I always found you to be, a faithful and considerate servant ; I would hardly have got on in this world and these hard times without such a friend, and in-return for your fidelity I will tell you a good deal about my affairs."

"Very well," said Tim, "nothing can give me greater satisfaction than to hear about my master and all that concerns him. I have no other friend after all but you, and I would be the most ungrateful man upon earth if I did not take great interest in your success."

Old Hawk then proceeded : " Yes, Tim, I tell you, that I know what you say is true, and you being worthy of my confidence, I have now to inform you that I am about being married, that is, I have made up my mind about the matter, and I hope you will in a few days have a mistress ; but let me tell you first what I have done this day, or rather what good fortune has befallen me. Whilst I was in the bank this morning I heard the glorious news that the father of young Lord Flare-away, from whom I got the post obit about ten days ago, had just dropped dead in a fit of apoplexy : he had been one of a large dinner party at Bishop Bloater's, and spoiled the fun and feeding by dropping dead at the dinner table before the feast was more than half over. I got a post obit for ten thousand, and all I gave the young rake was two thousand ; he had, besides, to pay Gripe the attorney a thumping bill of costs. And, by the way, that Gripe is a villain that must be closely watched ; he was to have given me half the profits on the young lord's bill of costs, and I have good reason to think that he cheated me out of a portion of it, but the truth will come out when I am calling in the post obit, which will be now in a few days. Only think of two thousand paid away ten days ago, bringing in five times the amount now ! Providence always favours the honest, saving, in-dustrious man ; but sure if we did not get an odd lift of that kind we could never get on in these hard times. I knew when I got the post obit that the old lord was such a drunkard and glutton that he could not live for any time, but it was the goodness of God that brought him home so soon. I calculated upon two or three years ; only think of ten days ! Come, Tim, fill your glass, and we will drink success to all post obit transactions."

Tim filled the glass, and said, " I don't exactly understand the meaning of these words, but what would you think, sir, if we drink to the memory of old Lord Flareaway ?"

"A capital idea," said Old Hawk, as he poured out a glass of good brown sherry, " let the toast then be, the memory of Lord Flareaway, and may all lords whose heirs owe honest men money soon meet the same fate."

" I say the same," replied Tim, and both swallowed off their wine.

> "He's gone—gone—and a new career
> Opens to me with the coming year."

"Now listen to me for a moment," said Old Hawk, "whilst I tell you what I am about to do, and ask your advice upon the subject. I know the change I am about to make is a very important one, and will add a good deal to our expense ; but if we expend in one way we can curtail in another, and I know that you will give me all the assistance in your power."

Tim replied, that much would depend upon the sort of mistress he would get, and added, that he was most impatient to hear her name.

"That," continued his master, "you shall hear presently, and if I mistake not you will approve of her as a person who will not expect too much. I have long thought of the matter, but the occurrences of this night have decided me ; Fogarty is an honest man, and I will have his daughter Kate in marriage ; she is a saving, proper young woman, who will be a good wife. I was in her father's house some time ago, when I heard her say that if she were a penny short of a hundred pounds she would not be any longer able to pay that sum, and that it was the pennies saved more than the pennies earned that made the money. Now to hear such wisdom from the mouth of a girl so young is rare in this age of extravagance and folly, and if I don't mistake much, the daughter of Fogarty is worthy of being united to the Norberry family ; but this brother of mine, who has such high notions, and whose son is now in college, will not consent to the alli-ance, and will do all in his power to prevent it, and more particularly as he ex-pects to get all my money, but I will disappoint all these expectants. Gripe, the villain, will be also disappointed in the accomplishment of certain plans he had laid for my ruin. You know he is attorney to that broken down spendthrift Colonel Dilkes, who has for many years been living upon the money of other people and keeping up appearances of splendour, regardless as to who will suffer in the end ; he has a daughter who has been forgotten by the world, although she has been all her life accustomed to go into what is called high society, and only think of Gripe proposing to me to marry her, with a view, no doubt, of her father and family laying hold of my hard-earned money ; but I shall disappoint them all : why, it would ruin a man, no matter what money he might have, to support a wife accustomed to such extravagance. It won't do, Tim, it won't do, and Gripe shan't pocket the poundage upon a settlement on the daughter of old Dilkes. Fill again ; here's ' Kate Fogarty of the Ram.'

> " I cannot tell the reason, but I really want a wife,
> And every body tells me 'tis the sweetest thing in life."

" Kate Fogarty of the Ram," echoed Tim, and both again quaffed their wine. "I approve highly of your choice," said the old servant, " I would like the beautiful creature for a mistress ; but, master, you are too old to marry so young a woman, and you know besides, that you should have her consent ; has that been yet obtained ?"

" No," said his master, " I have not yet spoken on the subject to herself or her father, for it was only this night I came finally to the conclusion of making her my wife. There can be no disappointment in the matter ; only think of the honour that will be done to Fogarty the inn-keeper, by an alliance with the Norberry family, and the certainty that she will have all my wealth after my death. The thing is quite certain. Kate Fogarty the barmaid at the 'Ram' transformed into Mrs. Norberry ! the thing is too tempting, there can be no disappointment ; and lest any fatality should occur, I will propose the matter to-morrow to the young woman and her father, but it must be kept a secret for some time ; Gripe must be kept in ignorance of every thing, the post obit shall be called in, and my papers taken out of his hands, before it is spoken of ; but what is to be done with old Shue ?"

" Why, of course," said Tim, " she will be a faithful servant to you and the mistress, as she has been to yourself ; and as you must have one, you would not think of putting her away."

" I don't know how that may be yet ; might I not as well marry the old Colonel's daughter, or some one like her, if I were to have servants to attend her ? I think Kate Fogarty, even when she becomes Mrs. Norberry, will not be above her own business, and that we can live very comfortably without the expense of a servant."

" I am sure, master," said Tim, " that that will be matter for future arrangement, and I can tell you from experience that your opinions with regard to the management of your affairs will be greatly changed by marriage. I was a very young man when I married Nancy Cassidy ; poor thing, she died after giving birth to a son in a little more than a year after our union ; and, in plain truth, I must tell you, master, that it cost me more that year than for other five years of my existence ; I loved the poor soul, and in honour of her memory I never thought of marriage again. It is now nearly thirty years since I came to your father's house, and I believe you have always found me a faithful servant ; the loss of my dear wife would have reconciled me to a fate much more unpleasant than to serve you."

" Oh," said Old Hawk, " you alarm me about the expense ; why, if the wife had lived you would have been ruined."

" I forgot to add," replied Tim, " that some way or other my means more than increased in a comparative degree with my expenses ; and I do believe, had God spared me my wife, I would have been better off in the world than I am, although I might have more care."

" Why, that is consoling," rejoined the master, " and I think it is now time that we should retire to rest. I feel that new scenes of an extraordinary character are before me ; that even in my old days I shall be blessed with a good wife, and if I had but one son to inherit my wealth, I would die happy. To-morrow Kate Fogarty, the handsome daughter of the honest landlord of the 'Ram,' shall be honoured by a proposal of marriage from the head of the Norberry family, and Gripe, the colonel, my brother, and the clan belonging to his haughty wife, shall be dissappointed. Good night, Tim ; not a word about this matter until it is all complete ; above all, old Shue is not to hear it ; I know that a woman cannot keep a secret."

Tim finished his glass of wine, and having stirred up the fire-wood in the grate, with a view to cast sufficient light about the apartment to enable his master to see the way to bed, he withdrew by a narrow passage which led to the rear of the house, to take his repose in the stable loft.

CHAPTER II.

AN ABDUCTION—AN UNEXPECTED RESCUE.

THE lofty summits of the Galtee mountains shone in golden splendour amidst the refulgent rays of an autumn sun, on an evening in the month of August, when a small detachment of military were seen in the distance, wending their way by a narrow road running through the fertile plains that mark the boundaries between Tipperary and Limerick ; the corn fields bore the yellow tinge of approaching ripeness, and being interrpersed with verdant meadows that undulated to the harvest wind, and played in waves before the refreshing breeze, the whole seemed as a sea of emerald and gold on which the refliction of the sun, from the polished arms of the little military party, flashed like a meteor, and formed a scene of peculiar beauty and grandeur. Upon the eastern ridge of mountains stood a party which consisted of two young lads, an elderly man, and four or five stout athletic fellows, who seemed in search of some lost treasure, or in expectation of meeting with friends in whom all their hopes and affections were centered. They appeared wholly regardless of the stupendous beauties of the surrounding landscape, and as the soldiers approached they changed their position, and sheltered themselves from observation behind some projecting rocks that formed the base of the summit from which they had been taking their observations.

"Father," said one of the young lads, " the soldiers have a prisoner tied upon a car ; oh ! I suppose Jack Ryan, our uncle, has been arrested."

"Very likely," replied the old man, " one sorrow never comes alone ; your uncle is arrested, and will no doubt be hanged at Clonmel, next assizes ; your niece has been taken away by villains who would have committed murder to accomplish their hellish purpose ; but had I been at home when they came, they should have drank my blood before the daughter of my only brother had left me ; and I think there is more to come : Ryan, I suppose, is arrested, and it is likely they have tortured him until he gave information about Patrick Butler being at our house, who was obliged to hide for putting a bad landlord out of the way. He, too, will be arrested and hanged, of course ; so that, my sons, it is a fearful thing after all to live in a country where the law affords no protection, because there is no confidence placed in it, and where it is administered by one party for purposes of cruelty and malice against another. But there is no use in bewailing our fate ; we would be better, after all, bad as the law is, had we obeyed it, and not left ourselves, in the power of the perjured informer and villain."

"Hush, father," said one of the young lads, "I don't think it is a man they have on the car; it is something very strange ; and whatever it may be it appears to be lifeless."

At this moment the soldiers halted, as if in doubt of the road they should go, and the party who had been watching them, believing that they had been observed, retreated though a narrow pass of the mountain that led to a village of five or six houses, which was so situated as to be inacessible not only to a car, but to any one on horseback, and which had often formed a place of rendezvous for the White-boys, who had some times previously been engaged in a crusade against an attempt

made to charge tithe on potatoes in Munster. Their object in visiting this strong-hold was with a view to summon aid to rescue the person so closely guarded by the military. Half an hour's quick pace over crags, and through defiles impassable to any but those accustomed to their intricacies, brought them to the first house in the village,'which was owned by a man named Lonergan, and here they unexpectedly met with six young men from a part of the country nearly forty miles distant, who had come over on a matter of business which should be transacted by strangers in that locality.

No 2.

Lonergan's house abutted on a portion of the mountain in which there was a natural cavern of immense extent, that was reached by a kind of sacred road, and here were often to be found fugitives from the officers of justice, as well as, those maimed or wounded in conflicts with tithe proctors, yeomen, barony constables, or occasional military detachments sent through the country to arrest notorious offenders. This cavern thus served the purpose of an hospital and depot for such insurgent forces as it was deemed necessary by Captain Rock to call together from time to time; and although the country people had access to it for the purpose of conveying provisions and admintsering relief to its occupants, it is a fact, that it was used for the purpose here stated for upwards of half a century before it was discovered. Its existence caused hundred of criminals to escape punishment, and as many innocent persons to be hanged in their stead. The respective parties were not long in explaining to each other the causes which had so unexpectedly brought them together. The leader or spokesman of those who were found in the house of Lonergan, having at once recognised in their visitors friends whom, according to the league that then existed amongst the Whiteboys, they were bound to assist, and from whom they could claim assistance in return, at once opened the business which brought himself and his associates to that part of Tipperary. "We understand," said he, "that you are greatly aggrieved by the villany of Bishop Fowler's land agent, old Tom Bateman, and we have come to level his house, and give him a warning to behave himself: the fellow is not yet fit to die, and we will not send him home at present ; but our principal business is, to level his new house, which we fear will be a difficult job." Now the history of Tom Bateman, or old Pipes, as he was called in the neighbourhood, was shortly this : Doctor Fowler, on being elevated to the See of Killaloe, appointed Bateman his agent, in consideration of receiving from him a considerable sum of money : he gave also in return, for his own immediate use, a portion of the church property, which was completely detached from the see, and situated in that part of Limerick which adjoined Tipperary, in the immediate neighbourhood of the Galtee mountains. Bateman, on getting possessed of these lands, immediately dispossessed the tenants, whose ancestors had resided on them for centuries, levelled their houses and erected a mansion for himself, which was more like a little fortress than the residence of a quiet country gentleman. Old Pipes was agent to several other landlords who had property in the neighbourhood of Dr. Fowler's church lands, and was noted throughout Tipperary for being most skilful in the application of the screw ; and such was the detestation in which he was held by the poor people, that none of them would venture to take a farm that might fall out of lease over which he was the agent.

To pull down the house of this old gentleman was the immediate business of the strange party who were assembled at the house of Lonergan, when they were met by those who had proceeded thither to obtain aid for the purpose of rescuing the prisoner who was guarded by the detachment of military, who were at that moment passing by the road that skirted the foot of the mountain. Promises of reciprocal assistance were given on both sides; but the party of strangers who were thus found at Lonergan's, required to know the nature of the expedition in which they were sought to be engaged, and whom they were called upon to assist to rescue. The old man stated that he did not know who or what the person was, but he could have little doubt that it was his brother-in-law Jack Ryan who had, with others, been accused of murdering a tithe proctor, who came to make a distress for potatoe tithe. He was sure he had been arrested, as the military had been several day in pursuit of him. "But," continued he, "that was not our immediate business ; we were out in seach of my niece, Kate Fogarty, from Dublin, who had come upon a visit amongst her friends in the country. She was a creature of great beauty, the May-flower was not fairer to behold, and although bred in a city, the sportive lamb was not more playful or innocent ; she came amongst us for a little to delight our hearts and gladden our eyes, but whilst myself and my sons were the day before yesterday absent at the fair of Holycross, a party of men came and carried her off from my house by force ; we know not where she is, and although we have been out in pursuit of the villains for the last day and night, we have been unable to find the trace of them ; we thought they were concealed about the mountain, and whilst we were anxiously watching the movements of every human being who came under our view, we saw the party of military coming towards us, guarding a prisoner tied on a car, whom we believe to be poor Jack Ryan, and our business now is not to allow him to be carried off before our eyes, to suffer a disgraceful death ; let us pledge ourselves to die to a man sooner than suffer such a disgrace to fall upon us."

"We are all ready," replied the strangers, "and if we die in the attemp, others will be found in the place from which we came to level the house of old Pipes and shave him into the bargain."

Lonergan, who was a man of much experience, having been present at more councils of war than even the celebrated Irish chieftain himself, advised that a vidette should be despatched in the person of a barefooted boy, who was celebrated through Tipperary for his agility, and who was generally employed in transmitting despatches from the occupants of the cave to their friends in various parts of the country. This extraordinary fellow, who was able to outstrip the fleetest horse at a long race, was called Cus-duvh, or Blackfoot, a name formerly given to any one who was in the habit of carrying messages of an illicit or private character from one party to another. Cus-duvh, who was an innocent looking sort of a fellow, was accordingly despatched, with instructions to cross the country with all speed until he came up with the detachment of military, and then, without seeming to manifest any great curiosity, put beyond all doubt who or what it was they were guarding so closely. The poor fellow set off at a moment's notice, and after a run of something more than four miles, he came up with the red coats, carelessly whistling an old Irish tune, and apparently wholly regardless of their business or destination. He cast an eye to the car, and, to his infinite surprise, he saw that the prisoner whom they were so closely guarding was a beautiful young woman, in a state of great exhaustion from terror and fatigue.

"Hallo !" said the sergeant who commanded the party, when he saw Cus-duvh, "can you tell us where the house of one Fogarty is ? we want to leave this creature safe at home with her friends, and the poor soul is so terrified she does not know this country at all, but we are determined not to leave her till we give her safe into the hands of her friends."

The poor fellow to whom the joyful news was communicated replied, that he would in less than no time have her friends, who were in pursuit of her, there, to receive her with joy, and he flew with the swiftness of an antelope back to the house of Lonergan, where he informed the assembly of the result of his mission. In a moment all were seen flying over the mountain in the direction of where the soldiers were, and when they came in view, the sergeant, apprehensive that an attempt would be made to rescue their charge, ordered his men to draw up in close column, and be prepared for the boys who were coming, if it should turn out that they were enemies. Cus-duvh flew on before the party as the bearer of a flag of truce, but O'Kelly, who was a prudent fellow, required that the main body should stand at a distance until some one would advance and be recognised by the young woman as her friend. This arrangement was promptly complied with, and the old man, accompanied by one of his sons, a promising, fine young lad, advanced to O'Kelly, who conducted them through his men until they were by the side of the car where the young woman was. The meeting between them was affecting ; the old man tenderly embraced his niece, and the young lad was almost frantic with joy at finding his cousin (whom he believed to have been taken away by the Dwkers, who were the most powerful clan in Tipperary, from whose clutches man or woman had never been known to escape), safely restored to her friends. The sergeant could no longer doubt that he ought to deliver up his charge to his new acquaintances, and the whole body of the countrymen at once came forward, and greeted the deliverers of the young woman with demonstrations of the most joyous affection.

"Why then," said the old man to the sergeant, "how did it come that you were the means of bringing back to us this dear creature, who is the only daughter of my only brother, Tom Fogarty, of the Ram Hotel, whom I have not seen for twenty years ? May the blessings of Heaven light upon your heads ; I will never repine at any misfortune that may befall me, now that I am able to restore to that brother, a treasure which he values beyond all the world."

O'Kelly, with all the frankness of a gallant soldier, proceeded to relate the facts connected with the rescue of Kate Fogarty from her abductors. He stated, that he and his party had been conveying two deserters to their regiment, which was stationed at Cahir, and wishing, on account of the heat of the weather, to perform their journey back to Thurles, where they were stationed, before the sun rose, they started from Cahir at midnight, and about two miles from that town they met, at a short turn of the road, a party of five or six men on horseback, having the young woman behind one of them ; the night was bright, and she having observed the arms of the soldiers glisten in the light of the moon, cried out to them for God's sake to rescue her, as she was carried off without her consent. The soldiers without hesitation closed upon the party, resistance was unavailing, and without injury being done on either side, Kate Fogarty was in a few moments safe in the hands of her deliverers, who had with them the car upon which the deserters had been conveyed to Cahir; upon this vehicle they placed her, and were returning in search of her uncle, when they were observed that evening by the party who went out in pursuit of her abductors, from a ridge of the Galtees.

The friends of Fogarty embraced the soldiers with the most unbounded affection ; and as it would be too far for them to march to Thurles that evening, every one of the party who had a house in the locality, insisted that one or two of them should take a billet with him for the night, promising them the best refreshment he could give. O'Kelly had an objection thus to separate his men in a mountanous district, with which they were not acquainted, although if a village was nigh, were all could be accommodated for the night, he was anxious to postpone his journey till morning. Old Fogarty, who was a comfortable farmer, with a good range of out-offices, settled the matter by proposing that all should proceed to his house, which was only three miles distant, and he would accommodate them in the best way he could. O'Kelly at once consented to this arrangement ; and Cus-duvh was despatched by a short way across the country with the joyful news that Kate was restored safe to her friends, and with directions to have a piper and plenty of "poteen" ready for the party as soon as they arrived. The poor fellow flew over hill and valley till he reached the house of Fogarty, and soon spread joy among its inmates, by the intelligence which he conveyed to them ; fires were instantly lighted, every pot and pan in the village was collected, and a flitch of bacon and a sack of potatoes were put in process of cooking ; a large cask of whiskey was provided, and every preparation was made to give the expected visitors a warm welcome. The military and their new acquaintances marched slowly along the narrow and intricate road that led to the house of Fogarty where they arrived in about an hour after Cus-duvh had given notice of their coming. By this time the sun had gone down below the horizon, the Galtees were dimly seen in the distance, a cool and refreshing breeze played along the vale ; Kate had completely recovered from her fright and fatigue, [and having bounded light and joyous from the car into the arms of her aunt and cousins, a more merry or happy party never congregated, even in Tipperary. The feast was by this time nearly prepared, a large barn was cleared out, doors were taken off their hinges, and being supported by turf cleaves turned upside down, they were placed from one end of the building to the other, and answered admirably for tables, all the stools, chairs, and forms in the village were collected, and seats having been arranged to correspond with the tables, the feast began. Old Fogarty took the head of the table, and had his neice upon one side, and her deliverer, the dashing sergeant, on the other ; the soldiers were promiscuously mingled through the country people ; all had their appetites sharpened by a weary march and a long fast, and take them all in all, it would be impossible to find a company more amply prepared to do justice to the repast. The bacon and cabbage and cakes of oaten bread came in, heaped upon wooden dishes, and he who was fortunate enough to possess a knife, was obliged to use it for the benefit of his neighbours as well as his own. The viands disappeared with astonishing rapidity, and when the task of mastication was performed to the full satisfaction of every one concerned, the temporary tables were removed, and the middle of the house being cleared of every obstruction, it was evident that preparations were making for a dance. But the most necessary preliminary to this amusement in those days, whsn teetotalism was unheard of, was copious libations of the mountain dew, and the cask of poteen was placed in the end of the building, the contents of which found their way through a wooden spigot into earthen pitchers, and from thence into egg shells, which were served round to the company by Mrs. Fogarty and the younger branches of her family, with that genuine hospitality and kindness of heart, which are almost unknown in the higher circles of society. The old man, who still continued his seat between his niece and O'Kelly, called for a bumper, and gave "the gallant sergeant and his men," with a hearty good will that was responded to not only by cheers, but by prancing and dancing as if the poor fellows had become frantic with joy. O'Kelly, who was a man of considerable education and knowledge of the world, returned thanks in suitable terms, and made some pointed allusions to the beauty of Miss Fogarty, which caused the maiden to blush, as she listened with surprise to the well-turned phrases of her handsome panegyrist and deliverer. Old Fogarty was not slow in apprehending the allusions made by the gallant sergeant, and expressed a hope that he would yet see his niece Mrs. O'Kelly, and see O'Kelly a captain. When the egg shells had circulated half a dozen of times, the piper commenced operations, and the feet of all the younger portion of the company were instantly set in motion; O'Kelly and Kate led off a country dance which was followed in quick succession by jigs and hornpipes, performed with a mirthful agility unknown to the slow scientific movements of our modern quadrille, or the heavy prance of a gallopade. The music and the dance were occasionally relieved by a song and story, and the night was passing by on the wings of joy, when a horseman was heard to dash at full speed into the enclosure. Jack Ryan, whose name and peculiar circumstances have been already incidentally mentioned, formed one of the party, and upon hearing the noise of an equestrian at such a time and place, he was seen to make his exit through a back window of the barn. O'Kelly was not slow in comprehending the meaning of his flight, but he seemed to pass over the circumstances unnoticed. All cause of apprehension was, however, instantly dispelled, upon a well-dressed, thick-set, muscular fellow, with a heavy brow and sinister cast of countenance, rushing into the barn, who was greeted with a hearty welcome, and shouts of "our old friend Queelan, all the way from Dublin." The cause of this unexpected appearance was quickly explained by him, to the infinite pain and embarrassment of some of the company.

He said he had been directed by the father of Kate, to proceed at once to Tipperary, and bring her back to Dublin without ever losing sight of her, o r delaying a moment; that the very morning she left home to pay the long promised visit to her friends in the country, a wealthy merchant of high family and connections had proposed for her in marriage; that great honours awaited the name of Fogarty by the alliance; and as no time was to be lost, she should proceed to the fulfilment of his mission at an early hour in the morning, when he hoped that Kate would be ready.

During the recital of this intelligence O'Kelly cast many an anxious look at Kate, whose face was crimsoned with blushes, whilst a pearly tear forced its way from under the long silken lashes of her dark blue eye to her cheek. Queelan having been regaled with plenty of the mountain dew, joined heartily in the fun and merriment that was going on; he listened with peculiar attention to the narrative of Kate's fortunate rescu,e and the cause that brought together such a heterogeneous assembly. He was then called upon for a song or a story, when he volunteered to give both.

He said, "I am well known to almost every one here, except these brave fellows, who have this day rendered such a signal service to the family of Fogarty; and erhaps some short account of myself may not be unentertaining to them. I was for many years the Captain Rock of the northern district of Tipperary, and have often led on the Whiteboys to do battle in the cause of their country; tithe proctors and parsons fled before me like the mists of the morning before a strong wind; but I was at length taken up, brought to trial, and having escaped, almost by a miracle, from being hanged, I quit the country, and am now doing well in a good public house in Thomas-street, in the city of Dublin.''

"Come, Queelan," said old Fogarty, " tell the sergeant, and tell us all, how you escaped on that occasion : I have heard wonders about your trial, but could never learn, the real truth of the matter."

" Well, then," continued Queelan, " many of you know the scourge that Disney, the land agent and tithe proctor, was, in this part of Tipperary, and notwithstanding all the warnings we gave him (for we never cut the ears off a tithe proctor or shot a bad landlord, without giving him timely notice to mend his ways), he still continued to ruin all the poor people with whom he had anything to do. At last it was agreed upon that he should be cropped and carded, and the task of performing those operations having fallen to myself and two others, we proceeded one night to his house for that purpose. We knew he was well armed, and that we might expect a desperate resistance if we attempted to take the house by force, and we had recourse to a stratagem that succeeded in putting the fellow into our power without much trouble. He always kept two or three blood horses which he prized very much, and one winter's evening after nightfall we got a large jackass, which we brought to his stable and turned in amongst them. The animals began to kick, squeel, and neigh, as if they were mad. The noise was heard by Disney, who was just after dinner ; the hall door was quickly unbarred, and out he came towards the stable. I placed myself as sentry, to prevent further egress from the house, the other two fellows seized Disney, and before he had time to utter a sentence, they stopped his mouth with a wad of tow prepared for the purpose, carried him off behind the stables, and commenced cutting off his ears. He was, however, armed with a dagger, with which he wounded one of the fellows in the breast, who would have been killed were it not that the point of the weapon was turned by a tobacco-box that was in his waistcoat pocket. Finding such desperate resistance made, the fellows, contrary to our original intention despatched him, without one of the family inside knowing what had occurred. Our business was then to conceal the body and leave his disappearance a mystery throughout the country, and for that purpose we carried it upwards of three miles to a bog, and sunk it in a bog-hole. When we separated, a thought came over my mind that one of my companions would turn approver, and that the other and myself would be hanged. I was near my own house, and recollecting that I had at home a fine black coat that belonged to a tithe-proctor, who, about two years previous, was stripped, and tied upon a wild horse, with a whinbush for a saddle, I went home for it, came back to the bog-hole, raised Disney out of it, took off a light coloured coat with gilt buttons which he wore, and with some difficulty put the black coat on in its place. I found that it fitted him admirably, and having put him back in the same position in which I found him, I returned home, and did not go to bed that night till I burnt every atom of the real coat, and melted the buttons into slugs. Well, to be sure the next day there was a terrible hulla-baloo about Disney ; no tidings could be had of him. He was a single man, and having dined alone on the day he was murdered, he was not missed by the servants for a couple of hours after he went out to the stable. No event ever occurred in Tipperary that caused such consternation. It was at first reported that having got possession of a large sum of money belonging to several landlords, he fled with it to France, but the finding of his body in the bog-hole in a few weeks after the murder, put the case in its true light, and an enormous reward was offered for the apprehension and conviction of the murderers. One of the villains who was at the perpetration of the deed, went to Dublin, turned ap-prover, and gave information against myself and our other partner in guilt, but he had fortunately fled the country some weeks previous, and was never since heard of. I was accordingly arrested in my own house by a strong body of horse and foot, and brought heavily ironed into Clonmel. The joy of the magistrates, parsons, and proctors throughout Tipperary exceeded all bounds, when they heard that the notorous Qaeenan, who was regarded as the Captain Rock of the day, had been arrested. The assizes went on in a few days after. Special counsel came down from Dublin to prosecute me ; the court-house was crowded to excess by the gentry of the county, and sentence of death was passed on me before I was tried at all. In instructing my attorney, I told him the only defence I had was an alibi, not only for myself, but the villain who was going to swear against me ; that neither he nor I had any thing to do with it ; but that I knew, as a matter of course, such a defence would not be believed, and that I gave myself up as a dead man. The trial went on, and the villain declared all the circumstances truly, with the exception that he put himself in my position as sentry on Disney's door, whilst I and the other fellow were murdering him. There were some circumstances of corroboration, and although they were slight, they were quite enough to hang any whiteboy in Munster. My witnesses were called up to prove that the informer was not near Disney's house the whole of the night or day on which the murder was committed, but they were all sent down off the table as unworthy of belief, my counsel shook his head, and seemed to say my case was hopeless ; the evidence closed on both sides, and the judge was about to charge the jury, when I said, in a tone loud enough to be heard by his lordship, 'Ask that villain, who is swearing my life away, one question.' 'No,' said the attorney, 'I will not instruct your counsel to ask another question.' 'What is it,' said the judge, 'you wish to have asked ?' 'Oh, my lord,' said I, 'that villain is swearing my life away for money ; he knows nothing of the transaction, as all my witnesses have proved, and it just struck me that I ought to ask what coloured coat or clothes the man had on him when he was murdered and put in the bog-hole, as he swears.' 'A very important question,' said the judge, 'and one that has not been put throughout the course of this trial. Call the approver.' The fellow came on the table and swore most positively that the murdered man wore a light coloured coat with gilt buttons ; there could be no mistake about it, as he had often seen him out fowling with a coat of the same kind, and that made him take particular notice of it. Several trustworthy witnesses, who were at the finding of the body were then called by the direction of the judge, and all deposed that the deceased had on a fine black coat, such as gentlemen would be likely to wear going to dinner. The counsel for the crown were wholly unprepared for such a question ; no one saw Disney go out of his house that night, and no one was able to prove what coloured coat he had on. The whole aspect of the case was entirely changed ; my counsel triumphantly called for an acquittal, inasmuch as the approver was rendered unworthy of credit, and taking his evidence away, there was nothing that could even fix suspicion on me ; the jury would see that the villain swore to the kind of coat that the gentleman used to go out to shoot in ; that the hand of Providence had almost miraculously interfered to save an innocent man, and that as soon as they returned their verdict of acquittal, he would call upon the judge to order the approver into the dock to be tried for perjury. His lordship was obliged to acquiesce in this new view of the case ; I was triumphantly acquitted, and the approver was actually put into the dock, more as a punishment for having bungled the case, than with a view to prosecute him, even if he were guilty. Having thus escaped the halter in this extraordinary way, I quitted Tipperary, and am now well to do as an honest citizen of Dublin."

O'Kelly, who, with all his comrades, had listened with the most profound attention to the story of Queelan, said,—

"Why was it that you reserved your defence about the colour of the coat to the last moment, when, if the judge did not allow your question to be put, you would most certainly have been hanged?"

"Ah !" replied the other, "I was a schoolmaster in my early days ; I have read a good deal ; 'Know thy opportunity,' was the saying of one of the seven wise men of Greece, and the man who has not acquired that knowledge knows nothing. Had that fact been disclosed, even at an early period of the trial, or before the counsel for the prosecution had closed their evidence, they would have got up a case to meet it, and it would have been of no value to me. I knew the question should be asked, and I took the only course that could save my life."

"Well, then," said the sergeant, "your story was so good we will now listen with equal attention and delight to your song."

"Very well," said Queelan, "then here goes."

> " Through sweet Tipperary
> I oft have been weary,
>   In leading the boys to do duty ;
> We disdained petty pelf,
> And all thoughts about self,
>   But made parsons and proctors our booty.
>
> " We made middle men fly
> As we raised the war cry,
>   And sure none but rack-renters can hate us ;
> We made land bailiffs quake,
> And the black sluggards ache,
>   When they thought to charge tithe on potatoes.
>
> " Oh, then, here's Church and State.
> May they ne'er separate ;
>   If they do sure our fun will be over ;
> And our captain himself
> Will be laid on the shelf,
>   Or go to sea, where he'll join the Red Rover.
>
> " Then though sweet Tipperary," &c.

The song, the dance, and the music having ceased, at the request of O'Kelly, at an earlier hour than some of the rest of the company wished, the place of revelry was transformed into one of repose, where himself and his men slept soundly till morning upon bundles of clean straw. At an early hour all the parties were in motion ; Kate was ready to proceed on her way to Dublin with Queelan, who was mounted upon an excellent horse. The parting between herself and O'Kelly was affecting in the extreme, and ere they separated he made her promise that she would write to him before her marriage, in case his regiment, who were daily expecting to leave their present quarters, did not reach Dublin before that time. She then with his assistance, bounded to the croup behind Queelan, who went off in a gallop. O'Kelly marched off at the head of his men, and both parties were followed by the anxious looks and loud cheers of the assembled spectators.

CHAPTER III.

CONTINUATION OF THE HISTORY OF BOB'S ANCESTORS—PREPARATIONS FOR THE MARRIAGE OF OLD HAWK.

OLD HAWK arose in the morning, sick for the first time in his life after the enjoyment of the previous evening ; the scenes of the night flitted over his memory like a troubled dream ; he appeared faint and weary, and was unable to take his usual breakfast. Old Shue observed the change in his manner, and expressed her surprise at her master not being able to breakfast ; she hoped that no tenant had run away from him with the rent, or any one died who owed him money.

His remarkable reserve and evident desire to conceal the thoughts that were crowding on his mind, only heightened the curiosity of his old servant, who could not rest until she went to blind Tim to seek for information on the subject.   There again she was met with a reserve that drove her almost frantic ; for she had sagacity enough to know that some change was contemplated in the household arrangements, which was to be kept secret from her.   In truth, she had always had some vague notion floating on her mind, that her master would one day or other make

her the legalised mistress of the old mansion, and partner of his fortune.   All attempts to extort information from Tim proved ineffectual, and her anxiety was kept at the utmost tension during the day, her master not having come home until nearly twelve o'clock at night ; and then he merely answered her interrogatories by monosyllables, and with an air of mystery that only increased her curiosity. He ordered her to go and seek for Tim, and then take herself to bed with all possible speed.

Tim, who was anxious to hear the news of the day from Old Hawk had at this
No. 3.

moment arrived, and as soon as Shue had been got rid of, the remnant of the bottle of wine that had been opened the previous night was placed on the table, the master and man drew their chairs together, when the former thus proceeded:

"I have broached the subject of the marriage to Fogarty to-day, who was, as you may suppose, delighted at the proposal; but by some strange fatality his daughter had proceeded at an early hour in the morning by the Fly, to Kilkenny, on her way to Tipperary, where she was to have remained for some weeks on a visit with her friends, but as I am anxious that no delay shall take place, I have directed her father to send for her, and have her brought back as soon as possible; a friend of his, in whom he can confide, will start to-morrow morning on the mission, and we may expect Kate Fogarty here within a few days."

"What did Fogarty say exactly, when you spoke to him on the matter?" inquired Tim.

"I will tell you," said his master," every word that passed. I walked into the 'Ram,' took Fogarty aside, and said, 'I remember your kindness to me last night, and although it was no more than what any honest man should do, it has brought me here to-day to carry into effect an intention which I had long since formed, and about which I have often wavered. I want your daughter in marriage.' The eye of Fogarty brightened up at this announcement, and his wife, who by my directions had been called into the room, seemed so overcome with joy, that I thought she would have lost her senses, and before her husband had time to make any reply, she said. 'Oh, Mr. Norberry, sure we could never have hoped for such an honour being conferred on our family; my daughter will be the greatest woman in Dublin; she will have her coach, of course, and

————"horses to travel up and down
With footmen all in livery to make a splendid show."

Oh! dear me, the Cavanaghs, at the other side of the way, who were always endeavouring to cope with us, will die with envy. Oh, the creatures, they have the curse of being poor and proud; they are always talking of their high family—of the princes of Borres, or some place like that in the country; but what will they say when they see my daughter rolling in her coach, and hear that she is the wife of Mr. Norberry, who is one of the richest men and best families in Dublin? why, it will drive the Cavanaghs mad; and then when they see the livery servants up behind the carriage, and sticks with gold heads on them in their hands, they will actually run out of the street. But what sad luck it is that my daughter is not here to receive this joyful news!' The foolish woman would have gone on at much greater length in the same strain, but that she was interrupted by her husband, who at once perceived that I was alarmed at such extravagant notions being entertained with regard to her daughter's future prospects and household establishment. Stop, woman,' said he, "stop your folly; you have idle notions about those things. Our daughter will have whatever her husband pleases, and no more, and whatever that may be, she will be satisfied, for she is one of the kindest and most gentle creatures in existence. I have never known her to complain of anything.' 'Poh!' rejoined the mother, 'what has Mr. Norberry been keeping up his money for but to spend it on a wife, and sure a prettier creature could not be decked out with jewels than our own Kate? Maybe a diamond necklace won't sparkle most brilliantly on her white neck, and feathers and pearls will look delightful over her raven hair!'"

"Ah, master," said Tim, "did you faint, or how did you bear to hear of such extravagance? I venture to say, before you go further, that the match will be broken off."

"Down in the valley come meet me to-night,
And I'll tell you your fortune truly."

"Hold your tongue," continued Old Hawk. "Hear me out. All that nonsense was only the dreaming of an ignorant woman. The father of Kate is a sensible man; his daughter is sensible and saving, she has no such notions as her mother. You know I told you before that I heard her say once, Take a penny from a hundred pounds and you are no longer master of that sum, and that it was the pennies saved more than the pennies earned that made the money. Oh no, Tim, I can never forget that. Let the mother rave away ; when her imagination cools down she will be very well pleased with having her daughter Mrs. Norberry, without coaches, servants, diamond necklaces, pearl head-dresses, and what not; besides, she must know that in the end her daughter will have all my money—that I am determined on, or at least I am determined that my brother or his graceless blackguard of a son, who is now in college, shall never touch a sixpence of it ; my wife and children shall have all."

" But tell me," replied Tim, " what did Fogarty himself say ? how did you part upon the business, or what arrangements are to be made for the wedding? But why do I talk of a wedding, till you have Kate's consent first ?"

" Don't talk of consent," said the master, " it would be impossible there could be a question about that ; the girl is young, her heart is disengaged, she knows I have money, and the hope of one day or another possessing it all, will soon decide her, besides, the father and mother will insist on it. I am going to purchase the wedding dress to-morrow. Come, Tim, take your wine, let us drink Kate's safe return and happy marriage."

Tim slowly filled his glass, and having drank the toast, he said, " Master, allow me to say one word by way of advice. Don't buy the clothes, or go to expense till after Kate's arrival, and that you have her consent ; something tells me there will be a break up in the business ; the creature is young and beautiful, and most likely somebody has made love to her before this, and the way with young girls is, that whoever has the courage to first declare his passion, is sure to be favourably received ; they generally get a preference. I remember when I made love t Nancy Cassidy, that in about a week after, two fine-looking young fellows were ready for her, but as I was the first to propose, she said, in gratitude to me, that she would have me in preference. Besides, master, you are so much older than she is, that I fear she will never consent."

" Silence, you old fool," said the master, whose temper had been ruffled by the evil predictions of his servant ; " silence ; I was a fool to have entrusted you with the secret, and here is the return I get for the confidence I have placed in you. What right have you to lay out such evil for me, when there are no grounds for supposing that it could occur ? I never mentioned a word of this affair to any one but yourself."

" Did you consult no friend ?" said Tim ; " or had you any to consult ?"

" No," replied the master ; and then stopping, as if his memory had run back over the dreary waste of a long life in search of one who could be honoured by the endearing name, but being unable to make such discovery, he said with a subdued tone, " No, no, Tim, I know no friend in whom I could confide but yourself ; but why, tell me, why do you distract me by prognosticating such disappointments ? for now that I have taken the thing in head, and have disclosed my intentions to the father and mother of the young woman, it would kill me if I were disappointed."

" Master, dear," said the affectionate old servant, " don't be either angry or sorrowful ; you admit I am the only friend you have in whom you could confide, and sure I would be the worst man in existence if I could deceive you, or say or do anything that would give you pain ; but I only took a common sense view of the matter, and said that the thing could not be certain until you had the young woman's consent, and that, afraid of disappointments, " it would be better not to purchase the wedding-clothes until after Kate's arrival."

! " Probably you are right," said Old Hawk, " and there is no use in laying out money till the moment it is necessary, but as to disappointment, that is quite out of the question."

"I hope so," said Tim, as he filled another glass of wine, and drew nearer to the fire. " But let me ask you, master, what is to be done with old Shue ? She seems as if in a state of distraction all this day ; did you tell her anything of your intended marriage ?"

"No," replied the master, "although she questioned me very closely about the matter, and I wish of all things she should be kept in ignorance of what has been going on."

"Ignorant of what is going on !" echoed a voice with a demoniacal shout, "I am no longer ignorant, I know it all ; and if I were to be roasted in —— for eternity, I'll have revenge."

"O may the Virgin of heaven protect us !" said Tim, "I have often heard that this old house was haunted, but I am now convinced of it. Master, dear, make the sign of the cross on your forehead, it will strengthen you against temptation, and guard you from your enemies."

"The cross won't do," continued the voice, in a shrill, grating tone ; "God or man shall not save him from my vengeance—mark that !"

Old Hawk shivered like an aspen leaf, shaken by the breeze, and Tim having rattled the poker against the bars of the old grate, as if to drown the unpleasant interruption, told his master to kneel down and say a prayer, and acting himself according to the counsel he had given, was on his knees in a moment.

Old Hawk paused, and said, "I remember not the time when I bent the knee to God ; I have not for nearly fifty years entered a place of public worship, nor have I ever during that time, that I remember, offered a single prayer to Heaven."

"You have been offering to —— all your life," continued the voice, in a tone of increased harshness and fury.

"Your evil predictions," said Old Hawk to Tim, angrily, "have been very soon fulfilled. Take care, old man, that you have not something to do with the fulfilment of your own prophecy."

"Oh, Father of Mercy !" said Tim, "let me finish my prayers. I never met with anything like this in the whole course of my life, since Ferguson, who was shot by Tom Grier, appeared in Gorteen house. I was a little boy at the time, and on a visit with the butler at Gorteen, when Ferguson came in, and we were all at the kitchen fire, drinking the first-shot of a charge of poteen that had been run that day. I saw his side all bloody, and his face as white as a paper ; he spoke to the butler, who was formerly an old servant of his, but his voice was so much more mild and gentlemanly than that of the master of the house or any other we were accustomed to hear, that we could have wished them all dead for the sake of improvement. And says he, when he came in, ' Don't be frightened, good people, it was the best thing ever happened to me to have been shot when I was, for had I lived a week longer, I would have committed a murder for which I would have been hanged. My business here,' he said, ' is to tell Keating the butler, who is a religious man, that attends church every Sunday, and has never told a lie, that I have a daughter by my first marriage at school in France, under another name, her parentage will never be discovered, unless you go to the house of Mr. Sheerin in Dublin, tell him to open an unregistered deed that I left there, and that will set all right. I have no more to say, further than that I am settled between the froth and water in the little lake at the bottom of the lawn, where I am to remain to the day of judgment and with that he left the room, before all our eyes in a flash of light ; and the truth is that his daughter who was most cruelly treated in France, because she had no money, and nobody knew where she came from, was brought home, and enjoyed all his fortune."

"Are these your prayers ?" said Old Hawk. "I have often heard that some prayers are very nonsensical, but such stuff as that I never heard. Come from off your knees ; let us search the house and see what is the matter. Where is old Shue ? is she gone to bed ?"

Tim arose, and having lighted a candle of the most slender dimensions, he and his master went on a tour of discovery through the old building to ascertain from whence the supernatural voice had proceeded. The sleeping apartment of old Shue was first visited, but she was not there ; every other nook in the house where she could possibly be concealed was searched, but without better success ; she was nowhere to be found. However, an inspection of the loft over the room where Old

Hawk and his servant were, led them to believe that the supposed apparition was old Shue, and that the voice proceeded from a hole which they discovered in the ceiling nearly over where they sat. Both were almost electrified with surprise, but Old Hawk manifested much more terror than when he had reason to think that he had been addressed by a ghost from the grave.

"I felt some horror," said he, " at your evil predictions, and I feel a presentiment of evils to come which I never felt before. I wish I had not thought of marriage ; I feel that my peace is gone, and that I will never be able to make money as I did."

"My dear master," said Tim, "be quiet ; sure it is not the loss of old Shue that would grieve you ; she may not be gone, but even if she be, you can do without her. You were speaking of discharging her when the mistress came home, and perhaps it is all for the better that she has discharged herself a few days before that time."

"Be it so," replied the master, " but the die is cast; married I must be, and the sooner the better."

The master and man then retired. for the night; the former to brood over the contending feelings that distracted his mind, and take a retrospective view of a life where there was not a single spot upon which memory could delight to linger, or one bright ray from the past to illumine the dreary though short way he had yet to tread. He was unable to close his eyes in sleep, and having arisen in the morning weary and distracted, he found that there was still no account of old Shue and he was obliged to make his way to the "Ram" to get his breakfast.

Some few days passed over in this state of anxiety and suspense ; there was no account of Shue ; Kate had not yet arrived, and Old Hawk was found late and early at the " Ram," where he was entertained by his intended matrimonial connections in a style of comfort to which he had hitherto been a stranger. In the mean time his wedding-dress was purchased to suit the taste of Mrs. Fogarty, who was in a perpetual state of hurry and bustle, and who wore an air of pride suited to the importance and dignity of the occasion. The daughter's dresses of course could not be purchased until she would be present herself to suit her own taste, but the old lady, in order to make the event more certain, caused Mr. Norberry to furnish his wardrobe with a handsome wedding-suit, calculated in her opinion, to make him look as brisk and as gay as a young man of five-and-twenty. His coat was sky-blue, with well gilt buttons ; white vest, ruffles, and tuckers ; pink cravat, top-boots, and small-clothes of drab cloth ; conical shaped hat, and white doe-skin gloves. Being tall and well made, when thus fitted out under the superintendence of Mrs. Fogarty, and having some fifty or sixty thousand guineas at his command, he was such as many young ladies of the present day, of much higher pretensions than the barmaid of an inn, could not find in their hearts to refuse.

It was on the third or fourth evening after the disappearance of old Shue, and when Mr. Norberry was dressed in his wedding suit, that Queelan arrived at the door of the "Ram," accompanied by Kate. Her mother flew to receive her with an exstacy of joy that completely overpowered the young woman. "Oh, my dear child," said she, " the greatest fortune that ever befell any people awaits us ; you are destined for the highest honours; if you only marry without hesitation our old friend Mr. Norberry, we will be all happy, you will be going in your coach, and the Cavanaghs, the vile clan, will die with envy. Come, my dear Kate, Mr. Norberry is inside ; let me at once introduce you to him as his intended bride."

Kate, who was sensitive and gentle in her disposition, and whose memory during the journey from Tipperary had been perpetually recurring to the comely form and handsome countenance of her deliverer, O'Kelly, felt as if the chill of death had crossed her heart, and all the fond hopes of a fervid imagination had been blighted in one instant. The simoon, laden with the mephitic effluvia of the poison tree of Java, could not be more destructive to the fairest flower, than were the last words of Kate's mother to the fondest hopes of her daughter. Still she was of that pliant, docile disposition, that would bear the most acute pain without repining' sooner than be the cause of pain to others.

She alighted from the "fly," which came from its terminus at Queelan's house in Thomas-street to the "Ram," sooner than give the young bride (for such she was designated by Queelan during the journey) the trouble of walking home, or put her to the expense of procuring a chariot, and was led by her mother to their state apartment, where Old Hawk was seated, dressed in his new suit. He arose at her entrance, and she stood before him in the proud consciousness that involuntarily marks the movements of the young and innocent, before sin or sorrow draws its curtain between them and Heaven.

Kate, although occasionally barmaid, or rather book-keeper, at her father's inn, was religiously educated, and wholly a stranger to the deceits and frauds of the world. She was remarkable for her beauty throughout Dublin, and this circumstance led the father to not permit her to attend the bar, except when such callous old gentlemen as Mr. Norberry were his customers. Perhaps a subject more worthy the pencil of an able pourtrayer of the human passions could hardly be afforded, than Kate standing before her venerable admirer, with her father and Queelan on one side, and her mother on the other, watching with fearful anxiety the result of an interview upon which, in their opinion, their future hopes and prosperity depended. There was a graceful pride and dignity in the mien of the maiden; the glances from her dark eye flashed like lightning upon the old man, who stood trembling before her, whilst a look of gentle reproach was turned towards her parents, which seemed to say, "Is this the fate intended for me?"

It is stated in oriental story, that the serpent is blinded when it gazes upon the virgin light of the emerald; and so, when vice beholds white-robed innocence in all its lustre and beauty, it falls back, blinded and abashed. Old Hawk stood for a moment under the lustrous glance of her eye, through which the workings of her heart found their way, then staggered back, and fell upon the seat from which he had just arisen.

"Oh! dear me, Mr. Norberry," said Kate's mother, "what can be the matter with you? You ate little or no breakfast this morning; you seemed to be in some trouble, but I thought the sight of poor Kate would have rejoiced your heart. Run, Biddy Flannigan, bring some water and pour it on his face, and unbutton his waistcoat, which that rascally tailor made entirely too tight for him; run, Biddy, run"—then turning aside to her husband, "Oh, Tom dear, he is dying! Oh, mercy be praised! if the knot had been tied an hour ago, what luck we would have had. But stop, he is recovering; he will live till the marriage is over, and then the sooner he goes the better."

Old Hawk had by this time sufficiently recovered to apologise by stating that some weakness had come over him, but that he was himself again.

The astonished maiden still remained in the same position, when her mother said. "Go forward, Kate, and give the old—why did I say 'old?'—give the gentleman your hand, it will give him courage to address you as his intended. Come, Kate, be a good girl, and do what your mother bids you."

Old Hawk, notwithstanding the mean and miserable habits of a life of avarice and deceit, had that pride within him which arises from the possession of wealth, coupled with being of a family that gave some names to the country who ranked amongst its aristocracy. He felt that he was humbled by the connection he was about to make, and rendered ridiculous by his exhibition before the barmaid of a hotel. Aroused by this feeling, he said, when he had sufficiently rallied to be able to speak, "This young woman seems to regard me with a degree of surprise and caution that I did not expect, but it is, I suppose, that bashfulness which arises from the novelty of coming into the presence of a man of high family and large fortune. Come, my girl, don't be abashed."

Kate, although disgusted at the rudeness of those expressions, merely said, that the novelty of the situation in which she was placed was calculated to embarrass a person of much more experience than herself.

"Come, come, Kate," said Mrs. Fogarty, advancing towards her daughter, and leading her over to Old Hawk, "give Mr. Norberry your hand; let us all be happy together; dinner is just ready, and when we shall have dined we will talk over this happy business." Then whispering to her daughter, "Oh, Kate dear, think of the diamond necklaces, the silk gowns, the head-dresses, and the coach. Come ladies and gentlemen, dinner is ready."

So saying, she led the way to the dining-room, where the tables were laden with the choicest viands the "Ram," could afford, and it was at that time celebrated for the best dinners given in Dublin. The feast went on, and the anxiety of Mrs. Fogarty to rally her daughter's spirits, and make her appear pleasing in the eyes of her admirer, was so intense, that she hardly knew what she said or did. Queelan formed one of the company, and astonished the whole party by a detailed account of Kate's fortunate rescue from her abductors in Tipperary, and a high eulogium upon the gallantry, manly bearing, great acquirements and handsome person of O'Kelly, her deliverer.

During his recital, the countenance of Kate varied like the glancing of the sun's rays through foliage shaken by the breeze, whilst playing upon the rippling current beneath. The countenance of Old Hawk, in which not a single outline indicative of one generous feling remained, was unmoved, although he saw plainly enough that her affections were centred upon another object, and that he could never hope to share even the slightest portion of them! but he said with a sardonic sneer, "Foolish young women like the sight of red coats, but come, Miss Fogarty, don't be thinking of the sergeant; you will be something more respectable as the lady of the rich Norberry, than seated of a snowy day upon the top of a baggage car; come my good girl, cheer up, the wedding must go on in day a or two."

"I like to hear that, Mr. Norberry," said the mother of Kate, " you speak like a wise man as you are; young girls, sure enough, like red coats, but the greatest misfortune that could befall one of them would be to marry or connect themselves with a soldier. I remember when I was a young girl there was a recruiting party, in the town of Fethard where I lived, and when I saw the fine sergeant, and the colours flying out of his cap, I thought the heart would jump out of me; and then when I heard the fife and drum, I wished to be out after them, and whenever they passed I used to be continually watching them out of the window, till at last the sergeant spied me, and in he comes without more to do and makes love to me. Says he to me, " Miss Ryan, you are a beautiful young woman, you would make the nicest sergeant's wife in the regiment; I will be marching out of this in about a month for Canterbury in England, so will you be ready to come with me?" The thing seemed so kind and so good natured, and he was such a good looking fellow that I could not refuse. 'Has your father any money!' says he; and faith it was he that had, for Tom Fogarty got three score goold guineas in his hand the day I was married. 'Indeed,' says I, 'he has money, and I am sure he will be very glad to give it to you with me.' 'Oh, say the, 'your father can't know anything about the business at all; there is a rule in the regiment that all the men must be married privately; do you be ready the day before I march, and be sure to have the money secured, we will want some of it on the way, and now that officers are falling in the war as thick as blackberries, I'll get a commission for the rest of it, and you will be an officer's lady.' Well, to be sure, I believed every word he said; I was making preparations for the day; I knew where my father had the money, and that I could lay my hands on it any moment; I fancied myself all as one as an officer's lady, when in less than a week after, the villain's wife and children came all the way from England after him, and I, Lord be praised escaped all sorts of misery. That's the way with the red coats; not one of them is to be trusted; no girl in her senses could ever think of one of them. Kate, dear, let this be a warning to you; but I know you have too much sense to require to be spoken to twice."

This story, told with such particular emphasis, did not fail to make some impression upon the mind of Kate, who thought it most likely that O'Kelly, who was much her senior, and who had travelled throughout most of the three kingdoms, was not without having his affections engaged by some other woman: besides, he had not made any declaration in her favour; he merely said, on parting with her

" I have the happiness of being your deliverer, and it is not too much to ask of you to give me some account of the person who aspires to the honour of your hand before you are married ; in a word, promise, in case you do not see me in Dublin before your marriage, to write to me."

This was all he said at parting with her, and upon turning the whole over in her mind, she thought it contained nothing that might not be said by a man who had been already married ; but then she remembered the hope expressed by her uncle at the feast in the barn, that he would see his niece Mrs. O'Kelly, and see O'Kelly a captain, and that nothing was said by him to negative such a hope being realized. On the whole, her mind was in that state of uncertainty when the counsel of a friend can most readily turn the scale of opinion one way or the other ; and she said, " Mother, you have had experience by which I ought to profit, and you know I must always take your advice."

The countenance of Mrs. Fogarty brightened up, and Old Hawk himself thought that the girl's heart was softened, and that her consent to the marriage would be obtained as a matter of course. Kate, to please her mother, disguised her feelings, and appeared to feel happy, so that the evening passed over in the utmost hilarity and good humour. Queelan told some of his Whiteboy adventures, which Mr. Norberry heard with apparent astonishment and horror ; he seemed to feel that his intended matrimonial connections were of that class which he mostly dreaded through life, for no man ever felt a greater desire to suppress outrage and violence by the gibbet and the halter than he did ; and the only occasion upon which he was known to subscribe to any public purpose, was towards prosecuting to con-viction persons charged with beating a tithe-proctor, and posting notices threaten-ing an agent with death if he came to collect rents upon an estate where he had himself a rent-charge.

Whilst the " quality" at the " Ram," as Biddy Flanagan, the pretty housemaid significantly called the company up-stairs, were enjoying themselves during the evening, the servants in the kitchen were, by the direction of Mrs. Fogarty, sup-plied with everything calculated to make them merry.

When all were assembled, Paddy, who was a poet as well as a minstrel, was requested by Biddy Flanagan to give something suited to the occasion, as she was most anxious to hear his opinion in verse upon the marriage of Kate. She said that she was almost tempted to write something for the occasion, for it was herself who could write; perhaps the company did not know that her mother kept a school in Francis-street, where she was doing well till she ran away with one of the volunteers who was billeted at her house.

" I'd like," said Jack Gormly, the ostler, who was one of Biddy's admirers, " to have a specimen of Miss Flanagan's poetry, I'm sure it would be beautiful."

" Come, come," said Biddy, " don't make so free till you're better acquainted. Let us hear what Mr. Barry can do."

" Ah!" said Paddy, with a shrug of the shoulder, " if I was amidst my own sunny plains at the cove of Cork, I would be in an atmosphere more suited to sing of love. I hate the smoke, and dust, and oppression of your dark city; the Muses never visit such an uncongenial region ; and if I attempt anything I know I must fail in it. But give me that tumbler of wine."

Paddy quaffed his wine, and thus proceeded with the following lay :

The time is come when none shall repine,
When cellars shall open and give up their wine,
That bards may drink to the maiden's dark eye,
And shouts of gladness ascend to the sky;

When the chorus, and song, and dance shall go round,
And music, and fun, and mirth shall abound;
When the bard shall sing of the beauteous flower,
Fit to adorn an Eastern bower.

Then here's to the maid with the dark blue eye,
Let our songs of gladness ascend on high,
But why should a flower so fair and so bright,
Be doomed to wither in shades of night?

Why should the happy, the youthful, and fair,
Be left to chill in the northern air?
And why should silver or gold have power
To tear the rose from its native bower?

But still there is hope that another is near,
Who will wipe away the pearly tear
That falls from the maid with the dark blue eye:
Then let songs of gladness ascend on high.

This effusion of the minstrel elicited universal applause; Biddy put the corner of her apron to her eye, as if to wipe away a tear that had been called up by the touching strain of the bard, and declared that she had never heard in her life

No. 4.

anything so nice and feeling as that which Paddy Barry had performed, to the infinite satisfaction of all.

"Pshaw!" said Jack Gormly, with a sarcastic sneer, "the whole meaning of the thing is, that a young woman is going to be married to an old man, and this I can tell you, that one of them would sooner marry an old fellow with money, than the finest young man in Dublin without it; and I'll give you a proof of the truth of this, for the thing happened to myself. It will also be seen that old fellows are easily imposed upon, and that when young women marry them they know what they are at." Here he gave a significant glance at Biddy, and thus proceeded with his story: "When I lived at my father's house in Clonthumper, I was as handsome a young fellow as you would see in a day's walk."

Here Biddy interrupted him by saying, "If all your story be as true as that, don't go further with it, for no human being will believe it."

Jack continued, "Ah! sour grapes says the fox, how bad I am, it is well known I never told a lie in my life." Here Biddy made the sign of the cross on her forehead, and called on the company to remember what he said, but Jack proceeded without appearing to notice the interruption.

"I was saying that it was well known that I was one of the handsomest fellows could be found in a day's walk; and there was Molly Gorman, a widow's daughter, who lived just beside us, who was a beautiful young woman, and she actually fell in love with me."

"Curse your impudence," said Biddy, "fall in love with you! no indeed, no woman in the world could fall in love with such a fellow the best day ever you saw."

"Arrah, Biddy, now cant you be easy; before I go further with my story, I'll hould you five goold guineas I have here in my pocket, that I'll be married to you before Christmas-day, and you are as handsome a young woman as a man could wish for; come now, if there be any one in the company willing to take me up, I'll post the rhino." Biddy held down her head, merely remarking, that no one minded anything he said; and there being no one to bet with him, not even Biddy herself, he proceeded with his story.

"But as I was saying, she fell in love with me, and surely I met her more than half way; preparations were actually making for our marriage, although I had hardly the marriage money in the world, when Molly went one Sunday to a place called Calumbkill, to see some friends of hers who lived there. She went to the chapel to be sure in great style, and there she met a rich ould farmer named Dooris, who had ten cows and a bull, a couple of horses, and a fine pillion, a good house hot and warm and full of every thing, with upwards of six score guineas stuck in the thatch, and what do you think but he makes love to Molly and tells her that he will marry her not caring whether she has any fortune or not. She heard all his riches, and says she to him, never thinking of me all the time, Come over and ask my mother, and sure whatever she wishes I must be agreeable to.' Well to be shure I heard all about it, and at first I was going to dhrown myself, but I went and took a large dose of whiskey, where there was a still at work next door to me and then instead of dhrowning myself, I intended to dhrown ould Dooris if I could catch him in a convenient place, but as luck happened I did not dhrown either. Well, the ould fellow paid some visits to Molly's mother, and every thing was arranged for their marriage; but the night before it, he rode over and slept at the widow's house, it being very late when the settlement was made. He rode off early in the morning to get the license; I saw him pass my door, and knew well what he was about, and that Molly would be married that day, so I took it into my head to go over and pay her a last visit. I went accordingly, and found her biling the tay kettle, to have breakfast ready when Dooris and his friends would come back with the license; and to tell the truth, when she saw me, a tear came into her eye, and she dhropped a fine new chiney cup out of her hand and broke it. "That is a bad sign, Jack,' says she. "what made you come near me this mornin'?' 'Why,' says I, I came to take my leave of you for the sake of ould times, and to tell you that a finer girl than ever you were is willing to marry me;' although, in point of fact, such was not the case at the time."

" I thought," said Biddy, with an air of exultation, " that you never told a lie in your life."

" Oh ! never," continued Jack, "except an odd one about women and game cocks; and I can tell you, Miss Flanagan, if you be catching me at every corner in this way when we are married, we will get on very badly together. But let me proceed with my story. Well, as I was saying, I tould her another was ready to have me. 'I'm glad of it,' says she, ' if it was only to put you out of harm's way ; but as you have come over to see me, I won't let you go till you take some break-fast.' 'Very well,' said I, ' we will part friends,' and I sat down at| the table opposite to her, when what in the world should we see but the face of ould Dooris at the window, and he looking in at us. 'Oh, murther,' says Molly, ' I'm undone, its all over with me, I won't have the fine house and the riches and all the fine dress ; you are an unlucky man,' says she. 'Never mind,' says I, 'all's not lost yet ; the ould fellow is almost blind, and may be he did not see me ;' so with that I made one bounce and up the chimney with me. I just put my head out so that I could watch ould Dooris till he got in ; he thundered at the door, and as soon as he got in I got out and jumped from the roof of the house into a cabbage plot which was at the back of it, and left Molly and her mother to manage him as well as they could. When he got in, 'Well,' says he, I had a narrow escape of you, it was lucky the knot was not tied ; give me back the money and the presents I gave you, and marry the fellow you had at breakfast with you.

'What fellow ?' says she ; ' are you mad, Mr. Dooris, or what in the world ails you this mornin' ?' 'Oh,' said he, ' I had sad luck to have ever met with you but it would have been worse if I had not detected you in time.' 'Whist, whist said she, ' don't awaken my mother that's asleep in the room after bein' up so late last night; if you think there was any fellow in the house, sarch it ; shut the door and sarch.' Well, the ould fellow fell to sarchin.' and to be sure I was not there ; he seemed completely bewildered, and did not know what to make of the matter. Molly began to cry, and run off to a neighbour's house, saying that she would not marry one who promised so badly in the beginning. Dooris, who was certainly in love with her, if an ould man can be in love, sat down at the fire, and began to muse over what he had seen. He took another bout at sarchin' through the house, but av course found nothin' ;' he sat down again and began to pause and think, when the ould mother, who pretended to be asleep, but hard all that went on, came up wipin' her eyes, and says she, 'Good-morrow to you both.' 'What both ?' says he, ' who are you talkin' to ?' 'Oh ! savoul deherih,' says she, ' I thought they were two of you in it;' and wipin' her eyes again, ' is there not two of you sittin' at the fire ?' 'No, no, woman, there is only myself in it,' says he, ' you are ravin'.' 'Oh !' says she, ' I broke my fast with scallions and salt this mornin', and when one does that they think they see two where there's only one.' 'Ah ! by this and by that,' says he, ' that explains everything. When I was going out this mornin', I was afraid of meetin' the hunger, and I ate a scallion and salt that was on the dresser; I did not go far when I turned back to give Molly some directions about the weddin', and when I came to the window and looked in, I thought I saw a fellow sittin' with her at breakfast. I was going to break off the whole business, and she is gone away cryin' to a neighbour's house I find I wronged her, so send for her and let us be all happy.' The weddin' went on that very evenin'. Dooris took the wife home with him, and from that day to this, ' good morrow to you both,' is a cant word, quite common about Clonthumper but the ould fellow, av coorse, never knew the meanin' of it."

" You never paid a visit to Molly after the wedding ?" said Paddy, with pecu-liar emphasis, as he run his fingers over the harp.

No, faith," says Jack, " for I had to fly the country in a few days after, abou u another matter which I need not mention, but you may be sure it was not for buildin' churches."

The night having waxed late, the company below stairs seperated, highly pleased with Paddy Barry's music and poetry, and the humorous stories of Jack Gormly.

CHAPTER IV.

MARRIAGE OF OLD HAWK—THE CELEBRATED DOCTOR O'LEARY—STRANGE VICISSI-
TUDES.

MRS. FOGARTY and all her household were on the *qui vive* at an early hour on the morning after Kate's arrival. The good old lady assumed an air of consequence and dignity suited to the importance and dignity of the occasion ; every heart was light and gay except that of poor Kate, who spent a sleepless night, resolving upon what course she should pursue, and whilst she was inclined to obey the commands of her parents, should they persevere in their determinaton of having her married to old Norberry, she thought it would be only right to fulfil the promise she had made to O'Kelly of writing to him before that event should take place. When she appeared at breakfast her mother was somewhat alarmed at perceiving that she was overpowered by a load of grief which she could ill conceal. She said ;

" Cheer up, my dear child, cheer up, and make us all happy ; Mr Norberry will be here presently, the dresses will be bought, and every thing will be ready for the wedding to-morrow ; and sure, Mr. Norberry is, after all, a fine-looking man, such as many a fine lady in Dublin would be delighted to get, and if it was for nothing but to make the Cavanaghs die of envy, sure it is a fine thing to marry him. Recollect, Kate dear, the coach and the footmen ; for although he may not buy you one now, he will hereafter, and you must in the end have all his money, and it is well known that he is one of the richest men in Dublin. Come, Kate, cheer up ; I tell you, you will get upon your right side the day you will be married to him ; for my part, I never heard of a girl have such luck."

" Indeed, mother," replied Kate, " I would do any thing under heaven that you would command me, because I know you have my happiness at heart, but the marriage cannot take place so soon as you say, for I am under a promise to write to some friends in the country before that time."

" Oh ! I see," said the mother, " you are dreaming about that sergeant, who, I would almost swear, is married already, and when I look back and think of the escape I had myself, it is enough to make me hurry on the matter without a moment's delay. Come, Kate, Mr. Norberry will be here immediately, and if you look so ill and melancholy when he comes as you do now, the match may be broken off, and we will be all ruined ; but, above all, the Cavanaghs will be laughing at us, for the report is all through the neighbourhood that you are to be married in a day or two, and if any disappointment was to take place we would be mocked and laughed at through all Dublin."

Kate entered into a long train of reasoning to show the impropriety of having the marriage celebrated so hastily, and concluded by a positive refusal to consent until she fulfilled her promise of writing to the country.

" Why, for that matter," said the mother, " you could write to the country this moment and get married the next ; all you promised was, that you would write before the marriage took place."

" That won't do," rejoined Kate ; " the condition is, that I shall not only take time to write, but to receive an answer ; and although in the end I will obey my parents, even if my life were to be sacrificed, I will not consent to be married until after I write to the country and hear from it too; besides, propriety and decency would be outraged by marrying a man after a few hours' acquaintance."

"A few hours' acquaintance!" said the mother, in an angry tone; "why, you must have known Nr. Norberry as a customer to our house for a few years; but what knowledge is there required of him beyond that of belonging to a high family and being, I verily believe, the richest man in Dublin? Come, Kate, you shall neither write or be written to, with my consent, until after the marriage takes place, and that will be the time to give an account of your good fortune, of the fine dresses and every thing else that will astonish all our friends in the country. The marriage must certainly take place to-morrow, if Mr. Norberry wishes."

"Certainly not to-morrow, mother," said Kate; "I am so far resolved about the matter, I shall not be married to-morrow," and she walked hastily out of the room.

Just at that moment Mr. Fogarty came in almost breathless, declaring that he was undone; that an order had come from the recorder of Dublin and three magistrates that his house should be shut up; that information had been given against him for having it open to all the Whiteboys and bad characters that fled from Tipperary; and in consequence a mandate had been issued for the withdrawal of his license and the immediate closing up of his inn; the police were below in the bar searching for whiteboy papers; in a word, they were utterly ruined, and he supposed that Mr. Norberry would break off the match when he found the miserable condition they had been reduced to.

Immediately after Fogarty had made this painful announcement to his wife, Mr. Norberry entered, dressed in his new suit, and assuming an air of gaiety to which he had been long a stranger. He saw the embarrassment and confusion that existed, and upon inquiring into the cause of such a sudden order of the closing of the "Ram," he found that the informations upon which the magistrates and recorder had acted were sworn by his old friends, the two watchmen, who had but some few nights previous offered their disinterested services in conveying him home when they believed he was in a state of intoxication. He called for the order that the police had for withdrawing the license of Fogarty and shutting up his house, and saw that it was signed by Samuel Bradstreet, recorder, Hans Bailie, Perceval Hunt, and Philip Cecil, aldermen and magistrates.

"I'll soon settle the matter for you," said Old Hawk; "these fellows are all in my power. There are two of them who owe me the lost gale of interest, and the third has given me a bond with immediate execution; leave them to me. But where is Miss Fogarty? I shall not interfere about the matter if there be the slightest delay on her part to marry me. I know how to act. If there be no marriage, there shall be no interference on my part, although I shall, in any case, assist in punishing these villainous watchmen, who are perjured robbers; leave them to me."

"Oh! my dear Mr. Norberry," said Mrs. Fogarty, "you are our only friend and protector; it was a kind Providence sent you to us; when Kate hears that you are our deliverer from such ruin and misfortune, she cannot hesitate a moment."

Poor Kate was here called down, and made acquainted with the sudden disasters that had befallen the family, and informed that it was in her power to relieve them in an instant from utter ruin, by consenting that her marriage should take place on the following day, or as soon as her venerable suitor should think proper. Her countenance assumed a death-like hue; she heaved a convulsive sigh, and in faltering accents, said—

"Father and mother, do whatever you please with me; I would die for your preservation. Let the marriage take place as soon as you wish, but I fear I cannot live till the ceremony is performed; I feel the chill of death about my heart."

She then fell almost lifeless into the arms of her mother.

Old Hawk who was unmoved at this affecting scene, then sat down and wrote he following note (the original of which the editor of these memoirs has in his possession), to Recorder Bradstreet, and the three magistrates who made the order for closing Fogarty's house :

"Mr. Recorder Bradstreet, Mr. Bailie, Mr. Hunt, and Mr. Cecil, I wish you all to know that I am the friend of honest Fogarty, whom you seek to ruin, upon what you would find to be false information, if you had taken the trouble to inquire about it. Withdraw at once your order for shutting up his house, and I will be security for his good conduct. You all know me, and are accustomed to see me write receipts, so there can be no mistake about this. Send back your answer without delay to—

"N. NORBERRY."

"Go," said Old Hawk, to one of the satellites of power who came to [execute the behests of the recorder and magistrates, "and show this letter to the gentlemen who sent you here ; take it round to them separately, and when they have examined it bring it back to me. If any of them doubt that the handwriting is mine, let them come here and satisfy themselves of the truth of the matter."

The fellow was off in an instant, and was not more than a couple of hours absent, when he returned with apologies from all the gentlemen for having had the misfortune to interfere with any friend of Mr. Norberry's, to whom they were under so many obligations.

When poor Kate had sufficiently recovered to be informed of what had been done, she felt that her father and his family would have been utterly ruined, were it not for the interference of her intended husband, and she thought she would willingly sacrifice herself for the attainment of such an object. She said—

"Mother, I consent. Do with me as you please ; but I hope that Heaven will soon put an end to my existence."

> "Joy's lingering ray is o'er ;
> This heart can ne'er awaken
> To one bright moment more.
> The hopes my soul had cherished
> Have withered one by one."

"Don't cry, my dear child," said the mother : "these feelings will soon be forgotten. Sure you ought to be the happiest girl in the world this day. Oh ! think of the coach, the silk and satin dresses, the diamond necklace, and all those fine things which you must have very soon. You will be able, besides, to give fortunes to your little sisters when Mr. Norberry is dead and gone. You will be all to nothing the richest and the handsomest widow in Dublin—not that I would wish poor Mr. Norberry to die soon, for I am sure he will make a good husband—a man near sixty. Oh ! why did I say sixty? I suppose he is only between forty and fifty. But a gentleman a little elderly cannot be expected to live as long as a girl of eighteen. Come, Kate, cheer up. You will be a credit to your family. The dresses will be bought this very day."

Kate saw that the die was cast, and that she might as well submit with a good grace. Preparations were accordingly made for purchasing the wedding dresses, and the second or third day after was appointed for the celebration of the marriage.

On the morning after Fogarty had been rendered so signal a service by Old Hawk, and whilst Kate was absent, a letter from O'Kelly to her fell into her mother's hands, and was thus prevented reaching its destination. Upon perusal of it, the old lady found that it breathed sentiments of the most devoted affection for her daughter, with expressions of surprise that she had not written to him any account of her intended marriage. He added that he would be in Dublin within two or three days, and have the honour of calling to see her. This circumstance induced the mother to hurry the matter to a close, believing that if her daughter either read the letter, or had an opportunity of seeing O'Kelly the alliance with old Norberry would, after all, most probably have been broken off. Directions were accordingly given to all the servants about the inn to state to any one who inquired for Miss Fogarty, that she was married and gone to the country with her husband.

The day appointed for the marriage came; and here a difficulty arose, which had not been previously foreseen. Old Hawk, who, although by his own confession he had not entered any place of public worship since he was a child, was a reputed protestant, and Kate being a catholic, it was necessary that they should be married according to the rites of the Established Church. Besides, it was highly penal then for any popish priest to officiate in any capacity whatever; in point of law, a priest was not supposed to exist in the country at all. Kate and her friends possessed all the bigotry and prejudice that oppression and persecution will ever produce, and next to the pain she felt at being compelled to marry such a man as old Norberry, was that of being obliged to go to a protestant church to have the ceremony celebrated. Yet all scruples about the matter should be overcome, and she was determined to brave the horrors of the double trial with all the energy and courage she could command. Old Hawk never made the slightest inquiry about the dogmas of any religion, or the faith that was in any man he dealt with, yet he had that intuitive horror of the mere Irish and their religion, which was peculiar to all his family. His notions of orthodoxy may, however, be judged of from a saying which he commonly made use of, namely, that "no man was religiously educated who could not turn all his sixpences into shillings."

Preparations for the marriage upon a scale of great magnitude were that day made at the "Ram." It was arranged that after the marriage ceremony had taken place in St. Patrick's cathedral, a second ceremony should be performed privately at Fogarty's house by the celebrated Doctor O'Leary of Cork, who was then in Dublin upon business connected with the publication of his review of the controversy between the Rev. Doctor Carroll and the Rev. Messrs. Wharton and Hawkins, who had, about that time, renounced protestantism, and become members of the Church of Rome.

The morning shone beautifully bright, and Kate, trembling and pale, was led by her bridemaids to the carriage, which was to take her to the cathedral, where, in a state of utter unconsciousness of what was passing, the indissoluble bond was sealed.

When the bridal party returned from the protestant church, O'Leary was in readiness to perform the ceremony according to the rites of his church. Old Hawk was peculiarly struck by the appearance of that singularly-gifted man, who, even in the dreary days of persecution and penal enactments, had the good fortune to win the affection of every man of every creed who had the happiness of his acquaintance, or read his works, which were then shedding light upon the darkness and bigotry of the age. It was said by Yelverton that he was proud to call such a man as O'Leary his particular friend; that his works might be placed on a footing with the finest writers of any age. They orignated from the urbanity of the heart, because, unattached to the world's affairs, he could have none but the purest motives of rendering service to the cause of morality and his country: and, had he not imbibed every sentiment of toleration from him. Then his good sense, unaffected piety, and extensive knowledge, gained him the respect and admiration of the learned, whilst his unbounded wit and unrivalled brilliancy of imagination made him the source of delight and entertainment to all who had the happiness of being admitted to his society. He was a native of the county of Cork, and related to the Fogartys of Tipperary, and Kate's mother, to give greater *eclat* to the festival, obtained his consent to perform the second marriage ceremony.

The astonishment of this celebrated ecclesiastic was beyond bounds, when the innocent, youthful, and beautiful Kate, and the hoary-headed miser presented themselves before him to have a contract already indissoluble, recorded again in heaven which should never have been entered into upon earth. He made no remark, but performed the ceremony with that dignity and grace which peculiarly marked the performance of all his ministerial duties. He grieved to find that the daughter of his relations had been united to a man who, besides the disparity of years that existed between them, was in a state of total darkness as regarded not only the practices, but the fundamental truths of religion. And he took occasion, after the ceremony was over, to dwell at length upon the majestic greatness of the catholic faith, the necessity of leading a life in conformity with revelation, the religious fidelity of the Irish people, who, amidst the most sanguinary persecutions and emaciating laws that ever disgraced any country, still preserved the faith as handed down to them by their fathers. "How," said he to Old Hawk, "did you like the cathedral where you were married this morning according to the rites of the protestant faith ?"

The other replied that he could hardly comprehend the use of so large a building, for it appeared to him that there was only a little corner of it fitted up—that all the rest was a mere wilderness; he had been there once before at the funeral of a friend; and had made the same observations; he wondered what had become of the congregation who originally filled it. This gave O'Leary an opportunity of launching out into one of those eloquent exordiums for which he was so remarkable when dealing with the evidences of the truth of that faith of which he was then the proud and distinguished defender, whilst he respected the speculative opinions of every other creed. He said, "That church in which you were to-day, stands as a proud monument of the piety and zeal of our fathers: the congregations which filled it in other days have had their blood shed and their properties confiscated, sooner than renounce the faith in honour of which that sacred edifice, and all the other splendid temples that adorned our land but are now in ruins, had been raised. The time, however, is not far distant, when they shall arise again phœnix like, from their ashes, in more than their original glory. Look around in the world, and you will see that sects, creeds, and empires, have flourished for a time, and then disappeared: the chosen followers of the Jewish dispensation are scattered over the earth, and have been without a kingdom or a temple since their overthrow by Titus; the empire of Greece, that gave the light of science and of letters to the world, has faded away; and the power, and glory of Rome, after persecuting the primitive Christians for ages, fell beneath the northern invaders, leaving, as it were, amidst the ruins of empires, and seated in the eternal city, the earthly head of the catholic faith, as a testimony of its durability and its truth; and that testimony will remain, no matter what revolutions may shake the kingdoms of the earth, until time shall be no more, and we shall all meet in the glories of a purer and brighter world, of which the clouded faculties of the human mind can form no conception, except that which is imparted by the light of revelation."

Old Hawk listened with astonishment to the eloquence and pathos of the language of O'Leary, and seemed half inclined to proclaim himself a convert to his creed; but dark shadows of the past flitted over his mind. He thought that the link which binds man on earth to heaven had been long since severed, and that he might as well continue as he was.

An early dinner, prepared for the bridal party, of which O'Leary partook, having been ended, a carriage and four blood horses drove up to the door of the "Ram" to take the unfortunate Kate and her hoary-headed husband to the county Wicklow, to spend the honeymoon.

Mrs. Fogarty ran to the window to see if the Cavanaghs were looking out; her vanity was not gratified, for there was not a stir in the house, no more than if they were all dead; but there was chalked on one of the window shutters outside, a representation of a blind man on crutches, and a young woman leading him.

"Well, well," said the good woman, "I knew it would come to that at last. Did any one ever see such an envious thing? I think they have all died of envy this morning; ha, let them cope up to us no longer. Oh! but there is the coach-door open, and the bride-maids are putting Kate in. Oh! dear me, but Mr. Norberry looks beautiful in his new suit, bought under my directions."

Kate was carried out half lifeless, and seated in the carriage; her husband stepped in after her, and the prancing horses tore up the pavements, as the postillions, who were decorated with white ribbons, drove of, amidst the cheers of a large mob, who were congregated about the "Ram."

"Hah!" said Mrs. Fogarty, "although the Cavanaghs won't come out to see they must hear that. But, hush! I see two or three of them peeping from behind the window-shutters: that will do; let them take that. I will go now and see that all the servants and neighbours who wish to come are served out with every thing they want. I am, to be sure, the happiest woman that ever the world produced."

FOGARTY EMBRACING HIS NEICE, AND TAKING HER FROM O'KELLY'S CARE.—SEE PAGE 12.

Human happiness is of short duration, and often, when we fancy ourselves secure in the possession of all that can gratify our wishes, dark clouds are hovering over our heads, which soon burst, and pour down upon us unforeseen misfortunes and sorrow. At the same time, if the history of all the evils that afflict us be traced to their source, it will be found that they have originated in our own faults and follies; and those only are wise who, by a careful retrospect of the past, can avoid similar errors for the future.

Mrs. Fogarty, though she had arrived at the summit of happiness, by getting the
No. 5,

object upon which all her thoughts and hopes were centred, accomplished; for she had not sufficient reasoning power to come to that most inevitable conclusion, that where any evil, real or apparent, is avoided by means inconsistent with strict morality, or by the violation of feelings dear to the human heart, there is only an avenue opened to a series of troubles, which would never fall in our way had we adhered to the strict principles of right, regardless as to consequences.

The coach which conveyed the bride and venerable bridegroom to the mountain scenery of Wicklow, had not been more than an hour on the road, when a fine young man, elegantly dressed, entered the Ram Hotel, and introduced himself to Mrs. Fogarty as Mr. O'Kelly, who had the good fortune to rescue Miss Fogarty from the hands of her abductors, in Tipperary; he hoped she was well, and begged that she might be informed of his arrival.

"Oh!" said the mother, unwilling to abruptly disclose the fact that her daughter had been that day married, "she is just gone to the county Wicklow for a little time, and will not return for some days."

"Tell her," replied O'Kelly, "that I called to inquire after her welfare, and to inform her of my own good fortune. A wealthy relation of mine in this city died within the last few days; he has left me a considerable portion of his property, and I am come to offer my hand and all I possess to your daughter, should she deem me worthy of her consideration."

Mrs. Fogarty seemed completely overpowered by this strange and unexpected news. Here was a young man, with wealth, the extent of which she was left to guess at—it might be, for all she knew, equal to that of old Norberry's; and as to family and connections, she was in doubt about them too; so that she began to think it might have been just as well if she had not been so precipitate in forcing on the marriage. She found, however, that concealment of it any longer would answer no purpose, and she said: "I have to inform you, Mr. O'Kelly, that my daughter was married this morning to Mr. Norberry, one of the richest men in Ireland; they have gone off to Wicklow to spend the honeymoon; she will have horses, carriages, servants, silks, satins, diamond necklaces, and everything else that a great lady can wish for."

O'Kelly's countenance during this extraordinary and unexpected recital portrayed the deep emotions of his heart; he was hardly able to articulate a word in reply, and after a long pause, he said: "Your daughter might be more happy in a state of comfortable independence than in the possession of those superfluities, which, after all, do not constitute true felicity in this world; but I could hardly credit that Miss Fogarty had been married so precipitately, had I heard the news from any but her own mother. There must be something connected with the matter which I have not heard. May I ask, where or by whom the marriage ceremony was performed?"

Mrs. Fogarty replied, that her daughter had been married in St. Patrick's church by the Protestant clergyman of the parish, and then by her cousin, Doctor O'Leary, of Cork, who happened to be in town.

"I believe," said O'Kelly, "it is too true. Where shall I see Dr. O'Leary?"

"He is here at this moment," said Mrs. Fogarty, "and is making preparations to start for Cork."

O'Kelly was immediately introduced to O'Leary, and had a long interview with him, during which he noted down all the particulars he heard from him respecting Kate's marriage, and then took his departure, evidently overwhelmed with deep grief. He returned on the following day, and having gained all the further information he could possibly obtain with regard to old Norberry, and the causes which led to his marriage with Kate, he again carefully noted all down. He had even an interview with blind Barry, the harper, who gave him no small quantity of material for his memoranda. He saw the father of Kate, who explained to him the urgent necessity which compelled him to give his daughter to old Norberry, and put into his hands the note which had been written by him to the recorder and magistrates, and which had the effect of saving him from ruin.

O'Kelly took his final departure not only from the " Ram," but from Dublin, and in order to connect hereafter the thread of this extraordinary history, it will be necessary to follow him on his travels for a short time. His regiment was ordered out to South America, and previous to his departure he purchased a company with the money obtained as a legacy from his friend. On his arrival at his destination he became acquainted with the family of a Spanish merchant, of Moorish descent, who had a daughter of exquisite beauty, who formed an attachment for him. They were married, and shortly afterwards, being ordered to India, he sailed with his wife, and on the voyage to Bombay she gave birth to a daughter. They landed safe in India, where we shall leave him with his regiment and family, until the reader will meet him again after the lapse of many years under circumstances of peculiar interest.

The day after Kate's marriage and O'Kelly's last visit to the " Ram," a Doctor Deering, who kept a private madhouse in the neighbourhood of Dublin, accompanied by Gripe the attorney, a young man fashionably dressed, and two desperate looking ruffians, alighted from a close carriage at Fogarty's door. The mad doctor as he was called (not from being insane himself, but from having driven so many sane persons mad who were given into his clutches), rushed in, followed by these desperate looking fellows, and asked Mrs. Fogarty if an old madman named Norberry had been stopping at her inn, or if she could give any tidings of him.

" An old madman named Norberry !" exclaimed Mrs. Fogarty, with indignant surprise. " You must be mad yourselves, gentlemen, to say such a thing. There is no gentleman of the name ever stopped here except the wealthy and the great Mr. Nipper Norberry, to whom, I am happy to tell you, my daughter Kate was married yesterday."

" Married yesterday !" said the fashionably dressed young man, who remained outside the door. " Married, does she say, doctor ?"

" Yes," replied Mrs. Fogarty, " my daughter has been married yesterday to the wealthy Mr. Norberry ; she will yet have her coaches and servants, silks, satins, diamond necklaces, and everything else that a great lady can wish for. I want to know, gentlemen, what concern is her marriage to any of you ?"

" I'll be——," said the young man, " if she shall have all these things in case I live. If I can lay hold of the old madman I shall soon put him up, and you may have your daughter back again to sweep the tap-room."

" Mercy be praised," said Mrs. Fogarty, " what does all this mean? My daughter never swept a tap-room ; she had no tap-room to sweep ; this is a very respectable inn for gentlemen, and no common tap, I can tell you ; every one knows the respectability of the Fogartys."

" Come, come," said Gripe, who till this moment had been silent, as if picking up all that passed to use as evidence upon some future occasion, " no more palavering, but let us know where this madman is ; for I can tell you, woman, that a commission ' de lunatico inquirendo' has been issued out against him."

" A what ?" said Mrs. Fogarty.

" A commission of lunacy," replied Gripe.

" Is it that you want to make out he is mad ?" rejoined the good woman. " Why, I can tell you that so far from being mad, he has given proof that he is one of the most sensible men in Dublin, for he has married my daughter, who is as handsome a girl as you would find in a month's journey ; not that I, who am her mother, ought to say it, but it is well known throughout all the city ; and if you were to see them driving off in a beautiful coach, drawn by four fine horses, it would do your hearts good."

" A coach and four horses !" said Gripe eagerly. " A coach and four horses ! Why, no greater proof could be given of the man's madness ; he who would look seven times at a shilling before he would part with it, to employ a coach and four even upon the occasion of his marriage (if he be married), is incredible, and can only be accounted for on the ground that his senses have forsaken him. We will have you, ma'arm, as a witness to prove that fact."

" Why, for that matter," said Mrs. Fogarty, " it was I who employed the coach

and horses, and hired the cottage in the   county Wicklow for a month, just to
vex the envious people. I know, to be sure, that Mr. Norberry will pay for all in
the end, but up to this he has had nothing to do in these matters."

"Worse and worse," replied Gripe; "your last account, which, no doubt, is
perfectly true, only proves that this doting old man is a mere tool in the hands of
low, designing people. Get me pen and ink at once, till I note down all you have
stated, and all the facts connected with this extraordinary case. You will be a
capital witness, ma'am, for you will be pinned to your first statement."

"You will note nothing here," said Mrs. Fogarty with indignation; "take your
selves away, gentlemen, unless you are going to make the house the better of you
and if you be, you are welcome to stop and say what you please; but this I can
tell you, that if Mr. Norberry were here he would soon make you beg pardon, as he did
the recorder and three aldermen who thought to close up our house without any
cause."

"Most important ! Do you hear that, Mr. Gripe?" said the fashionably dressed
young man. "He was actually the writer of the letter, of which we have heard so
much. Mr. Cecil fortunately took a copy of it, and we will make use of it on
the inquiry. No doubt can remain that the man is mad, is mad—perfectly mad."

"No doubt," replied Gripe; "no doubt whatever. But our business now is,
to lay hands upon him. Pray, ma'am," turning to Mrs. Fogarty, "what part of
the country Wicklow is this old lunatic gone to? I suppose your daughter, who
we have heard is devilish handsome, is gone to reside in the neighbourhood of
some gay young fellow who will pay attention to her when the old fellow is doting
about."

Mrs. Fogarty, who, notwithstanding her vanity and eccentricity, had a high
sense of moral rectitude, could no longer bear the rudeness and indelicacy of such
language, and ordered her servants to eject the gentlemen by force from her house.
Gripe, who knew that he had no authority to remain, withdrew along with his
friends before the command of the honest landlady could be executed.

It was by this time within an hour of night, and as it would be a hopeless task
to set off then to search amongst the Wicklow mountains for the bridegroom, they
all returned to their respective homes.

At an early hour on the following morning, the same party were on the road
leading to Delgany, in the neighbourhood of which place the object of their search
had been located. After some inquiry, they were pointed out the house where the
rich old man, who was married to the beautiful young woman, resided. Without
even deigning to announce their names or their business, they rushed in, when, to
their great disappointment, they found that Old Hawk was not there, but the
beautiful and unfortunate Mrs. Norberry was; and the terror caused by such a
visit, added to the deep anguish which had preyed upon her heart, from her return
to Dublin, so completely overpowered every faculty, that she fell lifeless from her
chair in a few moments after the intruders had entered her apartment.

The mad doctor, accompanied by the fashionably dressed young man, ran to her
assistance, but the latter was so overwhelmed with surprise at her surpassing
beauty, that he stood almost motionless, exclaiming, "It is no wonder that she has
driven the old fellow out of his senses." By proper applications, Mrs. Norberry was
restored to a state of consciousness, and then learned that the party who had come so
unexpectedly to visit her were in search of her husband, to have him put under
restraint as a lunatic, and she saw no prospect before her but that of hopeless sorrow and misery. She thought of the rashness and precipitancy of her parents in
forcing her to such an alliance, and she held down her head in a state of mental
agony, which is often supportable only from its own intensity, because it destroys
the power of feeling.

The absence of her husband was caused by a visit paid to him the previous
evening by his faithful servant and friend, blind Tim, who having heard some account of the proceedings which were instituted against him, and the search that
was being made for him, proceeded to apprise him of what was going forward.
He did not inform his wife of the unpleasant news he had heard, but went to town

in company with Tim, before the sun rose that morning, to take measures to avert the calamities with which he was threatened, and defeat the conspiracy that had been entered into against him.

The mad doctor and his companions returned to town in full chase of their prey They posted direct to the old house in James's-street, where they found Mr. Norberry, with poor Tim, arranging the contents of the safe in his state apartment, which has been already noticed ; bags full of gold, old deeds, bonds, and documents of various kinds, were on the table beside them. Gripe was the first to enter the room, and his eyes glistened with malicious delight when he beheld the treasure spread out before him, and just within his grasp. "Ho ! my old boy," said he," Caught at last ; it was Providence directed your movements. Why, we have got more by the accident of finding you in this place, and at such a time, than we could hope to obtain in years through the intervention of depositions, pleadings, bills in equity, and wat not. Come, sir, deliver up this money to me ; I am soli-citor to the *commission de lunatico inquirendo*; I just wanted funds to go on with the proceedings : I will, of course, be accountable for any overplus that may be left when the whole matter is closed. Come, Mr. Nipper Norberry, you have been long watching me, screwing me in costs and suspecting me of acting unfairly by you. I have got you at last, and I promise you, you will never get out of my clutches till you get into those of the only being in existence who can possibly be, a match for Gripe the attorney," So saying, he snatched up the bags of gold that lay on the table, whilst the terrified old man and his simple-hearted, faithful servant were motionless with surprise.

"Not so fast," said the fashionably dressed young man ; "that money should be left in my possession, as petitioner in the matter and heir to the property."

"Stop, stop," said Gripe, calling him aside, " you will ruin the whole proceedings if you interfere. What you see there is but a mere fraction of the old fellow's wealth. I know it. Recollect there will be an enormous sum wanted to pay the commisoners and the jury. You are not to know what they will get. The thing must be left to my management if you wish to succeed. If you don't place confidence in me, take the matter altogether out of my hands, and then you may easily guess what the result will be."

He to whom this pithy address was directed, saw that a villian such as Gripe was necessary to the accomplistment of the object in view, and he allowed him to take posession of the bags of gold.

"All right !" said Gripe in an extacy of delight ; " come, Doctor Deering, order your men to secure the lunatic ; put him under restraint at once ; he may commit violence upon hiuself. Bless my soul, how I grieve to see my old friend and client in such a position. But the ways of Providence are inscrutable, and we must all submit to the divine decrees."

"Very true," said the doctor; " very true, Mr. Gripe." Then in an under tone, "Remember my fees, and a provision for the support of the lunatic. Before we go farther, what am I to have out of the money in hand ? You know nothing can be done without me. Say a thousand guineas as per chance out of what you have ; we will arrange hereafter in proportion to whatever may be realized ; as you said yourself a moment ago, it is but a fraction out of his enormous wealth."

"Your demand is exorbitant," said Gripe angrily ; " you shall not have it."

"Then," said the doctor, " there is an end of the proceedings. If what I ask be the fifth part of what you have taken possession of this moment I will not ask any thing ; and I'll tell you this is no time to be talking about trifles ; I am, up to this moment, safe ; I made no affidavit. You know what I mean, Mr. Gripe."

"Come, come, my dear doctor," said Gripe, assuming an air of good humour, " you must have what you ask : tell your men at once to secure the lunatic."

The worthy doctor then made a signal to the two ruffians who stood outside. They rushed into the room in an instant, laid hold of the wretched old man, bound his hands with cords, and dragged him to the carriage which stood at the door, whilst he cried out, " My bags of gold ! my bags of gold ! Oh ! Tim, Tim, what has become of us !"

" Right so far," said Gripe, as the fellows placed him in the carriage ; "but this old man of his must be put out of the way for a time, to prevent story-telling. Aye, let me see—the poor lunatic will want an attendant in the madhouse; and it will be an act of great kindness and consideration to send his old servant to take care of him." Then, turning to Tim, " Come my old fellow, get into the carriage there with your master.'

" I will," said Tim, as a tear rolled down his aged cheek ; and he accordingly took his seat in the carriage beside his master and the two bailiffs.

The rest of the party entered another carriage, and all drove off to the private madhouse, at a place called Bopeep, on the Leixlip road, where Old Hawk and his faithful servant were left, under the tender mercies of Doctor Deering and his myrmidons.

CHAPTER V.

PREPARATION OF A DEED.—A PEEP INTO A PRIVATE MADHOUSE.—PROCEEDINGS UNDER THE COMMISSION OF LUNACY.—DEATH OF OLD HAWK.

Gripe and his client having left Old Hawk and his faithful servant secure in the asylum, returned to town to adopt measures necessary for their future proceedings.

" I have," said Gripe, as they proceeded on their way, " taken every precaution that human foresight and wisdom could suggest, to have this affair managed so as to render any hostile proceedings nugatory, if such should be instituted. My experience in such matters is of the utmost value in conducting a case where so much wealth is at stake ; and if I succeed in bringing the whole to a satisfactory termination, my expectations will be considerable."

" Considerable, of course," replied his companion ; " and probably it might be well to name a sum contingent upon that success."

" Yes," continued Gripe, " it might be well to do so, but we can arrange that point hereafter. I want, however, to know, before we proceed further, why it is that you have taken such pains to conceal your name in a transaction in which you are the principal promoter ? You know it cannot go on without your testimony, and, thus coming before the public, I doubt, too, but I may have committed an error that would vitiate the whole proceedings, by putting you forward in the petition under the name of Swingsnap instead of Norberry. By the way, are not you the full nephew to that poor lunatic whose fate we have such an interest in ?"

" Yes," replied the worthy client, " I am ; but, in fact, my name is Swingsnap, which I have taken from my mother, and by which I hope to obtain considerable property at the death of a family connection of that name in Scotland. Although, I am known, as a matter of course. by my father's name, it was by that of Swingsnap that I entered college. I knew what I was about when I prepared the petition in that name ; besides, I would not for any consideration have it thought, if exposure should hereafter occur, that a Norberry was the persecutor of a Norberry. It was always a maxim in our family, that " dogs don't eat dogs." A Norberry was never seen plaintiff in a suit against Norberry, When we want to bring a namesake to his senses, or drive sense or feeling out of him, as the case may be, we manage it in the name or person of another."

" I see," said Gripe, " all is right ; it was in the name of Swingsnap you entered college, and I suppose that that name also appears in the registry of your baptism."

" In both." replied Mr. Swingsnap.

" All right," rejoined Gripe. " I have arranged that we shall proceed to business on our arrival at my office in Saint Andrew-street, where Counsellor Muggleten is to meet us with the rough draft of a deed."

"Muggleton!" exclaimed Swingsnap. "Why, in the name of wonder, call in such a willy wagtail—such a nonentity as Muggleton? He is utterly despised as a barrister; he is, in truth, one of the most contemptible in the whole profession."

"Stop, stop," said Gripe; "my good young friend, not so fast; it is not talent we want so much, on an occasion of this kind, as fidelity. Muggleton is a man I can trust; he and I are members of a secret society, which, by the way, you must join very soon: a member of that society has never been known to betray the secret of a brother; besides, he is not by any means so deficient in acquirements as you seem to think. As to the preparation of the deed, it will be done under my own superintendence. I have had extensive practice in that way, besides having acquired a competent knowledge of deeds and pleadings generally whilst in the office of a conveyancer and equity draughtsman in London. You will find, Mr. Swingsnap, that I will manage the matter right, and if I get compensation according to my merits, my reward for conducting this business will be large indeed, but I scorn to drive a hard bargain with you."

The client of Gripe, who plainly saw the kind of man he had to deal with, could hardly forbear from telling him his thoughts, but he curbed his tongue, and merely said, as he cast an eye at the bags of gold that had that morning fallen into his hands: " Indeed, Mr. Gripe, I have already had a specimen of your disinterestedness in this transaction;" and then, affecting a smile, added, "I know your talents and experience, and that perhaps you are the only man in Dublin capable of conducting a case like this, and I am sure you will keep Mr. Muggleton from committing any mistake in the matter."

"That I will," said Gripe, with an air of self satisfaction; "I keep the bar in check wherever I am; I seldom employ one of them unless it is necessary to get his name to a pleading; I am in great favour with the bench, and I generally state my client's case myself. But, surely, Muggleton is not so contemptible as you imagine; he can make a plausible speech, has a little bit of the actor about him, and will state our case right well to the commissioners and jury who are to sit upon the inquiry."

"Very good, very good," replied Swingsnap; "don't for a moment imagine that I intended to dictate to you how you should conduct your business, or what professional men you ought to employ; all must go right in your hands."

"My dear young friend," said Gripe, assuming a look of kindness, " I have always had the highest opinion of your talents, integrity, and acquirements; that opinion has been fully verified by what I have lately seen of you. You are going to the bar yourself, and were I to give you but a portion of the junior business of my office, it would soon put you on the high road to fame. But I shall give it all to you; we will play into each other's hands. You will understand me better after a few interviews, when you get 'the wig' on."

"If I don't deceive myself I understand you perfectly this moment," said Swingsnap; "no doubt can exist that we may be useful to each other in many ways, even after we bring this business to a successful issue."

"No doubt in the world," replied Gripe; "and my future friendship and patronage will depend much upon how you shall act your part in this affair. For myself I think I may say that all my actions shall be purely benevolent and disinterested."

"Well, without running any risk of committing an outrage upon truth, I may say," rejoined Swingsnap, "that I shall not be far behind you in the exercise of those high moral qualities. We understand each other."

The worthy solicitor and his young client having at this moment arrived at the office in Saint Andrew-street, their self-laudatory conversation was broken off, and they proceeded at once to business, which, in their opinions, could not safely be delayed for a moment. They found Muggleton, who had a good voice, upon which he frequently dined with those who loved a song, sitting in the office of Gripe with his back to the door, singing the following verses—

I wish I was by that dim lake,
Where sinful souls their farewell take
Of this vain world, and half-way lie
In death's cold shadow ere they die.
There, there, far from thee,
Deceitful world, my home should be;
Where, come what might of gloom and pain,
False hope should ne'er deceive again.

The lifeless sky, the mournful sound
Of unseen waters falling round;
The dry leaves quiv'ring o'er my head,
Like man, unquiet e'en when dead!
These, ay, these shall wean
My soul from life's deluding scene,
And turn each thought, o'ercharg'd with gloom,
Like willows, downward tow'rds the tomb.

As they, who to their couch at night
Would win repose, first quench the light,
So must the hopes that keep this breast
Awake, be quench'd, ere it can rest.
Cold, cold, this heart must grow,
Unmoved by either joy or woe,
Like freezing founts, where all that's thrown
Within their current turns to stone.

Swingsnap stopped, and whispered in the ear of Gripe, " There is your man of business. It just corresponds with all that I ever heard of him."

" Don't mind," said Gripe peevishly; " I have already explained the matter to you. Ho! ho! Mr. Muggleton, how do you do? A delightful melody that! Sorry we interrupted you. Suppose after business amusement—you had the draft deed finished?"

" Ho! ho! my dear Gripe," said the counsellor; " how d'ye do? The deed is not finished. I could proceed no further without getting fresh instructions; and I was just about ordering a chaise to the door to post down to Bopeep after you, whither I knew you had gone; but you have fortunately arrived in good time.

" Mr. Swingsnap," said Gripe, without deigning a reply to what had been said about the intended posting excursion to Bopeep, and pointing to his client, who was standing in the middle of the room, " Mr. Muggleton, of whose talents and integrity you have heard me speak so highly, he is to be our counsel in this very heavy and intricate case."

The gentlemen formally saluted each other, when Muggleton commenced an exordium with regard to his talents and capacity in conducting a case of such peculiar delicacy, and so complicated in its various details. " It," he said, " required temper, talent, and ability, for the performance of the duties he had undertaken, and he flattered himself that he possessed some of those qualifications at least. No power under heaven could shake him from his purpose, or make him do aught but that which he intended to do, although, at the same time, no event that could by possibility occur should make him lose his temper. His great boast was, the command he had over himself, and he who conquered himself was sure to conquer others."

Swingsnap gave a contemptuous sneer, and cast a withering look at the stunted little egotist, who stood with head erect, evidently attempting to make his physical appearance correspond in some measure with the high mental qualities he had been describing, and said " I presume, Mr. Muggleton, that your clients must feel irreparable loss for every moment that you are unnecessarily absent from them; and undoubtedly your absence will be greatly prolonged by the kindness of your disposition in relating to us an account, most accurate, no doubt, of those high qualifications you possess, and which are so necessary in conducting a case like ours. We know you do so to satisfy our minds that we will be safe in your hands; but this is unnecessary, as we fully estimate your talents.''

Muggleton felt the full force of those sarcastic observations, particularly the allusion to the clients, for the poor fellow could not call to his mind that he had any, except two or three attorneys for whom he signed declarations at half price, giving them six months credit into the bargain, and he conceived at once the most

THE VISIT TO THE MADHOUSE.—SEE PAGE 44.

inveterate dislike to his new acquaintance; but he saw he could not afford to fall out with him, so he bit his lips, shut his good eye, and leaving the place of the other (which had been knocked out by the cue in a billiard-room) open, said nothing, and resumed the seat from which he had arisen.

"Come, come," said Gripe, " to business ;" and taking a key from his pocket, walked over to a large iron safe that was built in the wall at the opposite side of the room, opened it, and having deposited his newly acquired treasure within this fire-proof, and robber-proof magazine, took his seat beside Muggleton with an

No. 6.

air of satisfaction and delight that told how well pleased he was wi h the recent proceedings in which he had been engaged. Young Swingsnap stood watching the movements of Gripe, and casting a longing, lingering look after the bags of go d, as he shut the massive doors of the safe with a clank, and gave the key a particular twist, by which twelve strong bolts were sent out as guardians over the valuable contents within. He said nothing, but took his seat at the other side of the table, that he might hear the deed read, in which he had so deep an interest.

"What further instructions," said Gripe to Muggleton, "did you require from me, that should cause you to post after me, as you intended ?"

"Why," replied Muggleton, "there has been no specific detail of the property about to be conveyed; the particulars of which it consists must be enumerated. Chattels or lands cannot be conveyed with sufficient certainty without describing them."

"I have read some elementary works upon law," said Swingsnap, "and you are perfectly right, counsellor; the money got this morning must, of course, be counted over, and included in the conveyance."

The eyes of Gripe flashed like an enraged hyena, and he exclaimed with a furious tone, "No, sir; I thought we understood each other about that matter. Was it not agreed that the trifle alluded to should be *hors* the deed? Will it not be wanted for a purpose that was fully explained by me, and agreed to by you this morning? I fear, Mr. Swingsnap, I have been paying you encomiums this day which you did not merit."

"Why," said Swingsnap coolly, "if the deed be executed, the money will not be wanted for the other purpose, because you cannot get a man to execute a valid deed and have him declared a lunatic at the same time. That is the dilemma, Mr. Gripe. The property in question must be mentioned in the conveyance. If we cannot get the deed executed, why then the money will go to the purpose contemplated this morning."

"Why," said Gripe, assuming an air of good humour, "it is easy to manage the trifle in question without parchment. You forget that other claimants may come forward, and the deed would be indisputable evidence of the amount we should account for, and it would be nothing amiss that you, Mr. Swingsnap, a young man entering into fashionable life and a high profession, should have something that inquisitive people would know nothing about. I told you before to trust to my prudence and skill, or take the thing altogether out of my hands. I added, that all my acts should be benevolent and disinterested; you assented; and I am sure it is only necessary to recall those circumstances to your mind, and to show you that it is your interest alone I have in view, to induce you to abandon those mischievous crotchets, and leave the matter to my management."

Muggleton at once enlisted upon the side of Gripe, and added, that when a man had a solicitor of high honour and integrity, he should leave the whole conduct of his case in his hands, for many men had been ruined by following their own plans instead of the counsel of their law advisers.

"And not a few," replied Swingsnap, "have been ruined by their legal advisers too; but I submit at once to the wisdom, judgment. and discretion of my friend, Gripe."

"Ah!" said Gripe, assuming a tone of kindness, and looking with a hideous grin at Swingsnap, which he intended for a good-humoured smile. "I knew I was not mistaken in my young friend, who I am certain will shine in his profession, and yet occupy a seat on the bench."

Muggleton introduced the draft deed, which he read over to his clients, and after various alterations and additions, during which the temper and patience of Swingsnap were put to their utmost limit, it was agreed to; for he was obliged to submit to the arrangements dictated by his legal advisers.

This preliminary having been so far settled, it was arranged that the document should be given out for engrossment, and that the parties should meet on the second day afterwards, and proceed to the asylum at Bopeep, there to induce Old

Hawk to execute it. They were accordingly punctual to their appointment, and on a fine morning, as a crowd of shipping were under full sail, up the Liffey to he old custom-house, they were seen seated in an open barouche, going at full speed down the quay towards Queen-street, on their way to Old Hawk

Muggleton, who delighted in nothing so much as posting about in a hurry, under an apparent pressure of business, assumed an air of great importance, and requested that Gripe would again allow him to throw his eye over the deed as they proceeded towards their destination.

"Stop, my dear counsellor," said his friend ; " your impatience to be engaged in business at every opportunity that can be caught is no doubt most commendable but there is, after all, a time for everything. You may depend that all is right ; and, for my own part, I am much more inclined to philosophise upon the glories of this fine morning, and the surpassing beauty of the scene with which we are surrounded, than to speak of business just now. Can anything be more sublime and soul-stirring than to view the rays of the sun playing upon the full tide that fills, that noble river, in which are reflected the long line of buildings at each side, with the shipping seen in the distance, coming up, wafted from the bay by a gentle breeze ? I feel that such scenes as these always call up within me a strong divinity of soul, and I could almost wish that the spirit would burst its bonds, and soar into the glory, of which the scenes we now behold are but faint emblems. Yes, although tied to this world by its cares and pains, I have been always a truly moral man in my heart ; and, after all, unless we have morality as a gronud-work, our actions cannot bear the test of truth."

"You speak like a Christian and a philosopher," said Muggleton. "Your sentiments are worthy of a Bossuet or a Fenelon."

"You should add his acts, too," said Swingsnap, drily.

" Why, as to acts," said Gripe, " they are mere incidents which rise from the circumstances in which men are placed, and in ninety-nine cases out of a hundred they are not accountable for them ; but give me the man who loves the sublime and has a full sense of the goodness of the Deity, and I care not a yard of red tape about his acts, always premising that in every thing he does he will be sure to keep within the law."

" Your vocation has been mistaken," said Swingsnap ; " you should have been in the church ; if you were, you would ere now have mounted to the episcopal bench."

" Why," continued the worthy attorney, "a man can as well work out his salvation jostling through this busy world as filling the high place of a bishop, who has nothing to do but eat and drink and die of the gout. No, sir, my habits are too active for the life of a bishop, at the same time that I feel I have sounder morality at bottom than most of them."

"No great praise, after all," said Muggleton, who, from the time he was refused a perusal of the deed, had not ventured to edge in a word. " I think you are superior in many respects to all the bishops I have ever heard of ; and perhaps in your later days you may seek an asylum in the church, where you will have ample leisure to put in operation those high moral sentiments which do you so much honour ; men of your kind are much wanted in it at this moment."

" There are enough of good men there already," added Swingsnap ; "it is not, however, the men, but the establishment to which they belong, that has conferred so many blessings on the country. I am an ardent supporter of it, and I have no doubt that I shall yet render it some important services."

This conversation was interrupted by the arrival of the parties at the asylum, where Doctor Deering was at the gate to receive them.

" You see," said Gripe alighting from the carriage, " we are punctual as to time. It is one of the peculiar characteristics of my professional career, that I have never yet been known to break an engagement. Business for me, sir ; business, business."

" I fear," replied the doctor, in a low tone, " we will have a troublesome business with our *protegee*, and his stupid, obstinate old servant. He is of course, as sane as any man in existence. There is one circumstance in the case which can, however, be turned to good account ; the words 'my bags of gold, my bags of gold,' have hardly ever left his mouth since he came here, and that stubborn, stupid old servant of his is perpetually crying out, ' I'll prove the robbery the moment I get out of this.' "

" These are trifles," said Gripe. " The blind old rascal must get some hush money; that will soon bring him to his senses."

" I fear it won't do with him," replied the doctor.

" Leave that to me," added Gripe; "but we have come, as you have been apprised, to get the deed executed, so let's to business."

The worthy doctor led the way, and the party followed him through a long, dark corridor, to a small room paved with tiles, and admitting, through a grated window a considerable height from the floor, scarcely as much light as would enable the spectators to discern what the apartment contained.

" This," said he, pausing at the threshold of the door, "is a room peculiarly fitted to cases of this kind. I have had several distinguished persons here, who came to me in a far worse condition than our friend inside, whom I had perfectly convalescent in two or three months. You understand me. gentlemen ?"

" Perfectly," replied Gripe.

" Amongst those sent to me," continued the doctor, " were an old nobleman, whose son sought my kind protection for his dear father ; and a clergyman, whose wife and daughter sent him to me under circumstances of a very peculiar character. I fear there was not sufficient caution taken in the case ; and his malady was the most obstinate I ever had to deal with. He was a man of peculiarly sober habits through life ; and such persons are very difficult to cure. But the old lord, who was partially affected with *delirium tremens* coming in, was all right in a few weeks. You know what I mean ?"

" Oh ! my dear friend, not another word to explain your meaning," said Gripe. " I presume you were going to express your apprehension that this poor old man will present one of those inveterate cases which arise from long habits of sobriety and frugality ?"

" Precisely so," added the doctor.

" In that I think you are mistaken," continued Gripe ; " for it will be part of the evidence we will offer, in case we are forced to speed the commission, that the old fellow was latterly in the habit of getting drunk at night with his servant man. The servant woman, whom I have ready to be examined, is prepared to depose to that fact ; but if the deed be executed, there will be no necessity for it ; we will merely leave him under your kind protection, and you will know how to treat him: he is now very old, and cannot by possibility live many months."

" Precisely so," said the doctor; " and probably if the deed were executed, days would suit your purpose better."

" You are a man of business," added Gripe ; " I am certain that everything will be properly done in your hands. But you were I believe going to explain to us the peculiar construction of this room as a place of convalescence for your patients ?"

" Yes," continued the doctor, " it is entirely on a plan known only to myself. You are all friends, and I may confidentially state to you what its effects are. There is, immediately underneath the floor, a large reservoir of water, impregnated with a chemical preparation, that has long been a secret in my family, and this fills the apartment with a freezing air, whilst its soporific powers set the patient to sleep, who, upon awaking, is generally quite delirious, and cries out for warmth. This is the effect sought to be produced, and, as a matter of kindness, he is either brought out under a burning sun, with a thin cap on his head, or into an over-heated room, where he fancies he experiences great comfort from the sudden transition. This operation being gone through half a dozen times, even with ordinary regimen, is generally succesful. There is no appearance of coercion, restraint, or ill treatment of any kind ; and if even the servants of the asylum were to be examined as witnesses, they should depose that the patients are treated with kindness and indulgence. These, gentlemen, are the effects produced by confinement in this room."

"I suppose," said Gripe, "that course of treatment always effects a cure ?"

"Why, not always," replied the doctor ; "plaster for the head is the *ultimatum* ; but, throughout a long and succesful course of practice, I have very seldom been obliged to have recourse to it."

"Is the patient inside ?" said Swingsnap, eagerly; "I think we have heard enough about your practice ; let us see what are its effects upon this wretched old man."

"He is inside," replied the doctor, "in one of those balmy slumbers produced by the atmosphere of the apartment."

"Call him out," added Gripe, "for I should not like to go in after the information you have given us."

"Very well," said the doctor ; I merely wanted to show you how the patient was situated ; but I intend that we shall transact our business in my own apartments."

He then entered the cell, in a remote corner of which, stretched upon a miserable bed of straw, lay the man whose wealth had placed many of the lords and nobles of the land within his power, and who never paused for a moment to reflect upon the tears he had caused to flow, or the misery of which he was the author, whilst in the pursuit of gold. He was, however, now the victim of that grasping avarice which can only be satiated by wholesale gains, and is much more culpable than the slow process which leads through the dark and loathsome labyrinths of penury, extortion, self-denial, and deceit in the accumulation of riches ; for although the great bulk of mankind would seize, if they could, upon wealth in a moment, without going through any process by which it could be said, even in the eye of the law, to be fairly earned, there are few, very few, who have patience or perseverance enough to acquire it by labour, united to frugality and self-denial. Whether by the sweat of the brain or the brow, man, to acquire wealth, must labour ; and every man who is idle is a tax upon those who laboured before him, are labouring at present, or are to labour after him. Why mankind should universally condemn the miser, and concede their approbation to the anchorite, is an anomaly well worthy the consideration of the philosopher and theologian. The anchorite, who renounces the world and its wealth, and leads a life of self-denial, is an object of praise and admiration amongst many ; whilst the miser, who, with the means of gratifying all the wishes and wants incident to man, and of indulging in all the luxuries of the world, denies himself every thing, is an object of scorn and reprobation. Truly, if any thing can prove the philosophy and high moral qualities of any man, it is placing him in the enjoyment of immense wealth, without control or restriction of any kind, and then finding him pursue a course of frugality, prudence, and self-denial. The most worthless that the boiling over of great cities ever produced, if they get unexpectedly into the possession of wealth, will enjoy it with the bearing and assumed manners of the aristocrats of the day ; and those who are born to riches, instead of making money produce money, most generally squander what they received without labour or trouble. This would not be so, if they possessed some of the qualities which are so strongly condemned in misers. There is, therefore, something paradoxical in the matter, which philosophers or moralists have not yet accounted for, except upon the score of motives ; but it is with results, and not motives or intentions, that society has any thing to do.

The doctor returned, leading poor Old Hawk with him in a state of stupefaction or half consciousness, exclaiming, as he came out of the cell, " Oh, bring me to the heart ; I am shivering with cold."

" Yes, my dear sir," said the doctor, " you shall have your wishes gratified ; every thing that humanity and the most active benevolence can dictate shall be done for you. You know how kind I have been to you since you came here, and that kindness shall continue to increase as long as you are under my protection

Your friends are here, waiting to impart some good news to you, and to transact important business with you; but you must do every thing that they wish; we are all your real friends."

"Oh!" said Old Hawk, " have they brought back my bags of gold? And where is my wife? What has happened to me at all? And where, above all, is my only friend in this world, poor old Tim? Oh! Tim where are you? Where are my bags of gold?"

" Come, come," said the doctor, " we are going to make you happy; all will be right; come with me." And, taking him by the hand, he led him up the corridor, and across a court-yard, to his own apartments, whither Gripe and his friends followed.

On their way, poor Tim, who was looking through the bars of a window on the opposite side, saw the parties, and cried out, " Oh! my poor master, my-poor master; and the robbers who took all his gold. I'll swear robbery against every man of you the moment I get out of this—that I will; I'll transport the whole of you, for you are nothing but a gang of robbers! I'll put the law in force aganist every one of you—that I will."

" Ho!" said the doctor, " this is a troublesome intrusion. Hallo! Toby," calling to an athletie, ruffianly-looking fellow, who was seated on a bench under a shed, playing chess with a companion of similar appearance; " why have you that man in this side of the building? take him out of that quickly, and bring him to one of the rooms over the vapour bath." Toby and his playmate were on their way in an instant, and in a few moments afterwards the shrieks of the poor old man were heard as they dragged him mercilessly through a long gallery that led to the place which the doctor ordered him to be consigned to.

" Stop," said Gripe, " we may want this man; if the commission is to be sped we cannot well do without him; treat him kindly till we see how matters shall terminate."

" Toby," shouted the doctor, " bring back that poor man until further orders."

The willing satellites conducted Tim back to his former apartment, and then resumed their game with the most perfect *sang froid*, wholly regardless of the misery and sorrow, the pining hearts, the blighted hopes, and the ruined intellects of the wretched victims by whom they were surrounded.

The doctor and his patient were followed by the rest of the party into a reception room, magnificently furnished, which formed a striking contrast to the loathsome cell from which the wretched Norberry had been brought.

When Gripe entered, Old Hawk viewed him with a look of stupid amazement, as if uncertain of the identity of the person upon whom he gazed. At length he uttered, in a loud voice, " My bags of gold! my bags of gold!"

" Ha! my good, my dear old friend," said Gripe, assuming a lachrymose tone, " how my heart is grieved to see you in your present position! but a decided step was necessary to save the Norberry family from disgrace and ruin; it could not be tolerated that the very head of that family should form an alliance with the daughter of a low publican and plebeian."

" Stop," said Old Hawk; " where is my wife, where is Kate Fogarty? but, oh! my bags of gold, my bags of gold: return to me my money, and I will never think of wife or anything else; I will form no mean alliance; I am not married at all—at least I barely recollect it."

" A most important admission," said Muggleton; " let it be noted down; if there be no marriage, there will be no troublesome claimants from any other quarter, let it, by all means, be noted down, and put in my brief. I have always the foresight to catch the points necessary in my case."

" Come, my dear, dear old friend and client," said Gripe, " you do not appreciate the kindness that prompted this course; you do not know your real friends; just sign your name to this piece of parchment, and all will be well. Come, my dear old friend, there take the pen and sign your name opposit that piece of wax, and then you will get all your money and everything you want. Come, my dear Norberry, I have rendered you many a service in the execution of bonds, deeds, and post obits; just do what I desire you, and all will be right. You do not appreciate or understand the truly benevolent feelings which actuate your friends. Come, write your name like a worthy gentleman, as you have always been; don't dishonour the high name you bear."

"No," said Old Hawk, "never; I shall do nothing until my faithful servant and friend, Tim, is present; he witnessed the robbery that was committed, and he must also witness whatever else may follow."

"I knew," said Gripe, calling the doctor aside, " that we would be obliged to make use of that old servant; let me have an interview with him." Then, turning to Old Hawk, "my dear friend, just compose yourself for a moment; your faithful servant shall be brought to you; he is, I am told, a sensible man, and you will do whatever he advises you; just compose yourself for a moment."

"Come," said the doctor, "I may as well at once shew you the way to the apartment of the old servant." So, leaving the room, he was followed by Gripe, and both were in a few moments in the presence of Tim, who viewed them with amazement still greater than that manifested by his master.

"Ho! my man," said Gripe, "how are you? I am just after giving directions that whilst you remain here, everything shall be done to promote your comfort. The circumstances that have occurred appear strange to you; because, in the first place, you do not understand the benevolent motives which have directed these proceedings; nor can you forsee the wise ends for which they have been instituted. I have heard much of your integrity and attachment to your poor master. You have considerable influence over him, and we wish you should exercise it to induce him to write his name to a document, the purport of which, as a man of unimpeachable honour, I declare to be, to save the Norberry family from disgrace. You heard of your master seeking to be married to the bar-maid of a public house, kept by wily, crafty, cunning, low-bred people, who would be his ruin. We want to take him out of their hands, and it is only by signing the document in question that it can be done. You must prevail on him to do so; but then if you should fail in that, I will draw up a statement of facts for your perusal, which you will of course depose to on oath at an inquiry which is about to take place. Come, my worthy old man, your integrity must be rewarded." So, taking from his pocket a leather purse, he emptied its contents upon the seat of the window, at which Tim was still standing, gazing into the court-yard, as if in hope of catching another glympse of his master. The poor fellow saw sixty golden guineas told over, and again placed in the purse by Gripe, who, with an air of kindness and condescension presented it to him.

"There," said the doctor, as the hand of Gripe was outstretched with the proffered gift; " there is an act of generosity and benevolence that ought to make you value the friendship of Mr. Gripe, and convince you that all he is doing with regard to your master is founded upon the purest and most disinterested motives."

The faithful and incorruptible Tim, whose actions throughout a long life were prompted by the emotions of a kindly heart and innate rectitude of principle, which had never been corrupted by worldly pursuits, took the purse containing the proffered treasure from the hand of Gripe, and, summoning all the strength he could command, he flung it at his head, and struck him a stunning blow on the right eye. And, by the way, sixty golden guineas, rolled up in a leathern casement, would form a pellet, that, when projected from a strong hand, few would like to be visited by, even for the sake of its contents. The blow had a terrific effect upon Gripe, who staggered back and would have fallen, were he not supported by the doctor, who was dumb with amazement at the scene he had just witnessed.

When Gripe recovered sufficiently to collect his thoughts, he said, in rather a gentle tone, " I see that this wretched old man is as mad as his master, but he is of that dangerous class of lunatics that requires quite a different mode of treatment; leave him for the present, and we will consider hereafter what is to be done with him." And then turning round, he walked back towards the apartment where he had left Old Hawk and the other gentlemen. The doctor picked up the rejected gift and followed him.

When they entered, Swingsnap inquired where was the servant, or what was the result of the interview with him?

Gripe, whose disappointment far exceeded his rage—for he was a man who had perfect control of his temper—pointed to his swollen eye, with an assumed smile: "There," said he, "is the result of the interview with that dangerous old maniac, he is much worse than his master. There is nothing left but to speed the commission."

"I will have him sent to one of the rooms over the vapour bath," said the doctor.

"I think," said Gripe, "I will manage to have him brought out of this, and placed in Newgate in Dublin, as a dangerous lunatic. I will make a deposition before the magistrates at Mountrath-street police office as soon as I go into town, and we will get rid of him in that way."

"I have a precedent here in one of the books I brought with me," said Muggleton, "from which you can both frame your deposition, and draw up the form of a commitment, to have ready to be signed by the magistrates. I always come prepared for any contingency that may arise. I am always ready to meet the collateral points as well as the main branch of my case."

"If all the world thought as highly of you as you do of yourself, you would soon be lord chancellor," observed Swingsnap with a sneer.

"Come, come," said Gripe, "this is no time for either bandying compliments or indulging in malicious jokes; we have business of much more importance to think of." And he placed his hand upon his eye, which was causing him much pain.

"Hallo! Toby," said the doctor, "take this old gentleman back to the place from whence he came, put a collar and waistcoat upon his old servant, who is raging mad." Then, turning to Gripe; "I fear the plaster to the head must be adopted."

Toby and his companion executed in an instant the behests of their master; and after some further consultation amongst the parties, and such medical advice as the doctor thought applicable to the damaged eye of Gripe, which was beginning to assume a serious appearance, they took their departure for town, discomfited and cast down, in the same vehicle which had borne them out in triumph.

On their arrival, a deposition and committal, with regard to blind Tim, was prepared by Muggleton, and on the following day Gripe attended before the magistrates of Mountrath-street to swear to it. He had with him a certificate from the doctor, which stated that the individual in question had been sent to his private and peaceful asylum, where repose and quiet were so necessary for its inmates; but that his instanity being of that boisterous and dangerous character, it was unsafe, as regarded both the poor man himself, and the quiet, kind-hearted class of servants necessary for the establishment, and unjust to the other inmates, who were all of the highest order of respectability, to allow him to remain there any longer, and that he ought to be sent to one of the public prisons, where treatment would be pursued which by no possibility could be adopted at the retired and happy asylum of Bopeep.

Armed with these documents, and presenting an eye with a purple circle round the orbit, which radiated into hues of varied yellow, Gripe came before Messrs. Smullet and Ember, the presiding magistrates at Mountrath street, to render his depositions, with a view to have the unfortunate but faithful Tim removed to the side of Newgate allotted to dangerous lunatics, where hundreds have lived and died in a state of wretchedness and misery without parallel, who were at first driven to paroxysms of despair by the cruelty, the rapacity, the deceit and injustice of their fellow men, but who, by kindly treatment, or one honest voice raised in their behalf to rescue them from such a fate, might have lived amongst society in possession of the glorious gift of that reason which loathsome dungeons, mismanagement and neglect could not fail to destroy.

"Make way there, constable make way," said Mr. Ember, as the parties advanced towards the bench. "Bless my soul! gentlemen, how do you both do? But what accident has befallen you, my dear Gripe? When I was a practising lawyer, you were one of my best clients. How grieved I am to see your eye in such a condition; what in the world is the matter with you?"

"Indeed," replied Gripe with a tone of humility, "I am not the first who has been made the victim of an indiscreet generosity and ever active benevolence. The documents I have with me will explain the matter better than I can but I may shortly mention that a most unaccountable misfortune has befallen one of the oldest clients and best friends I had in the world—both himself and his servant have become insane, and under the directions of some members of his family, I had both removed to the asylum of Dr. Deering, which is an earthly paradise. The in-

No. 7.

sanity of the master is of an idiotic and harmless kind, but that of the servant is of a most dangerous character. I went yesterday to place a considerable sum of money in the hands of the doctor, for the benefit of both, with directions that their comforts should be strictly attended to, although that indeed was wholly useless," (this was the only part of the tale that was true), " when the wretched man seized the purse of gold that I was handing to the doctor, and flung it at my head ; here" (pointing to his eye) " are the effects of it ; and here are the documents that will further explain everything."

" A singular case, indeed," said Ember ; " but we are in the habit of hearing such extraordinary cases every day that we are hardly surprised at anything. You, however, have the consolation to know that you received that injury whilst in the performence of a most sacred and meritorious duty. Pray be seated, gentlemen ; be seated whilst I read over these papers. Muggleten, how do you do ? it is a good many years since we were serving our terms together in London ; you see I am tied here to the magisterial bench ; I am almost sorry that I gave up my practice at the bar for it."

" I trust," said Muggleton, addressing the worthy magistrate, " I shall see your worship elevated still higher. Your high legal attainments and practice at the bar would have entitled you to be chief justice of the king's bench."

Ember graciously nodded assent to the complimentary statement made by his friend, and then continued with an air of great gravity to read over the papers that had been put into his hands by Gripe. When he concluded, he slowly raised his head, elevated his spectacles from his nose to his forehead, and remarked that it was a singular case indeed ; he had met, he believed, in one of the year books an account of a master and man having become mad simultaneously ; but it was afterwards discovered, in the course of a complicated law-suit which grew out of the matter, that they were brothers, although the fact had been a secret for upwards of fifty years

" Such a discovery," added Gripe, rather testily, " won't be the result in this case."

" I don't presume, by any means, to say it will," replied Ember ; " your course, however, is clear ; sign this deposition, and I shall sign the committal which appears to have been drawn up with great care, and the poor unfortunate man must be at once removed to the lunatic side of Newgate, as the place best suited to him."

" The committal has been prepared by me," said Muggleten, with an air of self-satisfaction ; " I manage matters with temper and caution. I take care never to lose my temper, so that I come coolly to the performance of all my professional duties."

" The document does you great credit," replied Ember, nodding graciously.

Smullet, the other magistrate, who seemed to be making amends for want of the previous night's sleep, opened his eyes when all was over, exclaiming " What case is this before the bench ?"

" Nothing," replied his worthy brother magistrate, ' but the committal to prison of a dangerous lunatic."

" Oh, that's a mere matter of course," grunted Smullet.

The documents having been duly executed, Gripe and his friend left the office to make preparations for speeding the commission, and Ember despatched two or three confidential constables to convey poor Tim from Bopeep to Newgate ; and before the sun set that evening, they had executed their commands.

" There is nothing for it now," said Gripe to Muggleton, as they passed from the police court into the street, " but to speed the commission without a moment's delay. Your brief is nearly ready ; you must make a truly pathetic statement ; but all will depend on a good jury ; they must be corporation men—fellows who love good dinners. and have no visible pursuits or means of existence except what arises from their pay as yeomen, and fees as jurors."

Muggleton suggested to Gripe that the corporation roll should be submitted his inspection before the jury would he struck ; as he had an opportunity of meet ing many of them who were good singers, and were repeatedly asked to parties at which he, too, had the honour of being entertained.

"Your suggestions," said Gripe, "are well worthy of consideration. Ascertain, therefore, in the first instance, how many of our own picking can be placed on the jury; but don't throw up any signs, lest they might be mistaken by a freemason, if amongst them: get a majority of 'us' by all means, but throw up no signs when delivering your address."

"You speak like a man of sense," replied Muggleton, "and I shall attend to your suggestions with the utmost care and caution; but is not there a hope that old Norberry will yet sign the deed? Doctor Deering thinks that when the plaster is applied to his head he will consent."

"Oh,——the plaster," said Gripe; "the commission, after all, is the better course of proceeding; it must succeed.

The gentlemen then proceeded to the office in Saint Andrew-street, where it was agreed to meet at the lunatic office in Chancery-lane on the following morning, to make arrangements for summoning a jury and proceeding with the commission. Muggleton, Gripe, and Swingsnap were accordingly, early in their attendance at the office, where a jury list, to the satisfaction of the parties was prepared and despatched to the sheriff, with directions to have them summoned for the following Monday. A liberal fee accompanied this request, and the sheriff lost no time in having summonses served upon the worthy corporators, whose names had been marked upon the list sent in by Gripe.

At an early hour on Monday morning, all the parties concerned were in motion. A number of fellows with carbuncled faces, and dressed in shabby black, were seen entering a narrow, dingy, dirty-looking passage in Chancery-lane, which le to the place appointed for proceeding with the commission of lunacy. The commissioners were punctual in their attendance, and took their seats on the bench with an air of gravity suited to the occasion. There was a good attendance of jurors; many who did not receive summonses came upon the speculation that some of those who did, might, by some fatality have been absent; and when the chosen number were sworn, the others left the court with long faces, as soon as they heard the commissioners declare that, as a mark of respect to the feelings of the highly respectable family upon whom a most direful affliction had fallen the proceedings should be conducted in private.

All preliminaries being thus arranged, Muggleton ostentatiously unfolded a huge brief, on the back of which a fee of fifty guineas had been marked, and was proceeding at once to state his case, when Gripe rose and walked behind the backs of the jury, who were seated in two rows upon forms removed a considerable distance from the bench: as he passed on, each man thrust his hand behind him, which was met by that of Gripe, then hastily withdrawn, and afterwards carelessly thrust into the capacious pocket of his waistcoat. This process having been gone through, the worthy jurors closed into a narrow circle, and after a short consultation, the foreman, with a good-humoured smile, and a peculiar leer of his eye, announced that they were ready to hear the statement of the learned counsel.

Muggleton then rose with great gravity, and having adjusted a large pair of spectacles which he generally wore for the purpose of hiding his bad eye, proceeded thus to address the commissioners and the jury:

"Gentlemen, I am here in counsel in the case of Norberry, a lunatic, and Swingsnap, petitioner; and if I find myself completely overpowered by the weight of the duty I have to perform, and the feelings which the recital of so painful a case must call up within me, I know that I am addressing gentlemen of humanity, station, and experience as jurors, and that I may confidently calculate upon your indulgence. There are cases where the advocate becomes involved in the profundity of his own thoughts, when he contemplates the inscrutable ways of Providence in visiting the most virtuous, dignified, and upright of the human race with afflictions which are almost too much for humanity to bear. But this collateral contemplation, if I may use the term, would only lead to metaphysical abstraction, and a theological inquiry which however highly edifying and instructive in itself, would only turn our minds away from the issue you have this day to try. Of all the afflictions that can possibly tbefall any individual or family, it is that of insanity.   It is one of those visitations occasionally sent by an all-wise Creator for purposes known only to Himself; and our duty is to meet such an infliction with virtuous stoicism, and to give our warmest sympathis to those who are either immediately or remotely 'the victims of 'such a malady.   There is one melancholy consolation with regard to the unfortunate maniac that renders his condition in some degree less painful than that of his family and friends, and that is, his unconsciousness of the malady with which he is afflicted. And, gentlemen of the jury, whilst I implore your sympathies for the unfortunate gentleman who is the object of the present inquiry, I beseech you to extend them in as peculiar degree to his sorrowing friends, some of whom will be examined as witnesses here this day; nay, I would say, extend them to myself, for I am a man who feels poignantly for the sorrow of others; and whilst I thus address you, I may confidently assert that my anguish is at least fully equal to that of my highly respectable clients, for whom I appear here this day.   I find I am almost unable to proceed ; but gentlemen, you will excuse my weakness—the sympathies of the man have overcome whatever little forensic power belongs to the advocate—and if you do not extend to me your kind indulgence, I would be just in as melancholy a condition as the unfortunate old gentleman whose case we have come here this day to consider. You will perhaps, be inclined to ask me, before I go further, who are my clients in this matter, and at whose instance this commission has been sued out ? and I might reply, that the whole of the high family of Norberry, with all its collateral branches are my clients ; but those who are immediately concerned in the present proceedings are Mr. Swingsnap, the nephew and heir of the lunatic—his father and family, and that highly upright, benevolent, and respectable solicitor, Mr. Gripe, who had been for many years the law agent and bosom friend of the lunatic; as well as the confidential adviser of other branches of the honse of Norberry.   His affliction and anguish at the calamity that has befallen his friends are beyond the power of description.   The painful task of examining him here this day as a witness will fall to my lot; and I fear it will be too much for me. Extend, then, I beseech you, to my client, Mr. Gripe, the same sympathy which a moment ago I begged might be exercised with regard to myself ; and any you may then have left is due to my young client, Swingsnap, who has to go through the painful ordeal of a petitioner, in a case where his uncle is the lunatic.   You may then look remotely towards the various branches of the Norberry family, who, I am instructed to say, are deeply pained at the calamity that has fallen upon their kinsman.   Do not think, gentlemen, that I am following the hackneyed track of making an appeal to the feelings and passions of a jury—no such thing. If even my instructions were such, there exists no necessity for doing so in the present case, because I have the honour of addressing gentlemen of the most enlarged sympathies, noble minds, and active benevolence, who require not the adventitious aid of an appeal from an advocate to enlist all their feelings in the cause of humanity and truth.

"Gentlemen, having now said so much by way of preliminary, permit me to open to you the facts of this extraordinary case. You have all heard of Mr. Nipper Norberry, remarkable alike for his wealth and eccentricity, but still bearing that high name in the mercantile world worthy of the family to which he belonged. He led a very frugal and retired life, and most probably the misfortune that has befallen him would never have occurred were it not that some infernal trap was laid for the unsuspecting old man, by the owners of a tavern were he was in the habit of dining. These people, it is supposed, administered some dose to him that deprived him of his senses, with a view to get him married to their daughter; and they have actually given out that a marriage has taken place. Be that as it may, gentlemen, it was observed that soon after Mr. Norberry began to visit the house in question, and that these artful, cunning eople set their snares for him, his habits became totally changed, and from leading a life of the most perfect sobriety, he began to indulge in the use of strong drink, and was in the habit of going to bed in a state of the most beastly intoxication, his pot companion being no other than his own servant man, who, I must inform you, ha also become deranged, and is now confined in Newgate as a dangerous lunatic."

Foreman of the Jury—"Oh! the case is quite clear; the two old fellows set themselves mad drinking. There was Alderman Clinker, with whom I had many a fine dinner, and he died roaring mad. from the effects of brandy and claret, which he would swallow off like small beer."

The worthy counsel continued :—

" There can be no doubt, gentlemen, but a sudden transition from habits of frugality and sobriety to those of intoxication must have had a considerable effect upon both master and man; but I fear the malady with regard to both is seated much deeper, for had it arisen from the mere temporary use of strong drinks, being deprived of that indulgence, and under the kind and skilful treatment that both have since received at the hands of one of the most able and humane men in his profession, Doctor Deering, would have effectually cured them; but both cases, although different in character, are perfectly hopeless. You all know, at least you have heard, that Mr. Norberry was deeply affected by the *auri sacra fames*, and it is one of the peculiar characteristics of his complaint, that he is perpetually calling out for bags of gold, and alleging that he has been robbed of a large quantity of that precious metal. The malady of the man so far corresponds with that of the master, that he declares himself ready to swear to any thing he says about the gold and the robbery; but in every other respect he is perfectly outrageous in his conduct, and has been removed to that portion of Newgate allotted to dangerous lunatics, where he will remain, I suppose, for life, having no property out of which the expenses of speeding a commission of lunacy could be paid; but he will have the happiness of being under the care of Doctor Deering, who is owner of the private asylum where his poor master is so kindly treated, he being also physician to the prison. I would here turn away from the direct thread of my narrative to pay that eulogium to the professional and private character of Doctor Deering, which both so richly merit; but, being personally known to you all, it would be a work of supererogation to do so; and the feeble praise that I could bestow would only detract from the merits of the name which carries with it its best eulogy. Yes, gentlemen, the name of Doctor Deering will, I predict, be hereafter gratefully remembered by posterity. But, to resume the painful thread of the facts connected with this distressing case, let me at once inform you that the first witness who shall be produced to you will be the female servant, who lived for many years with the old gentleman, and whose veracity and integrity are above all suspicion. She will depose to you that for some time before the malady with which her unfortunate master is afflicted had become publicly known, he was in the habit of sitting up all night drinking with the old servant man, and talking about some young woman, with whom he fancied he was in love."

A Juryman—" I suppose this is the daughter of the tavern-keeper to whom it is alleged that he is married? I see—I see the whole case."

" You are right, sir," continued Muggleton; " and permit me again to express the delight I feel in addressing a jury composed of men of such high moral worth and intelligence. You know my case—you anticipate my very thoughts—and my address shall be consequently very brief. Well, gentlemen, being, by some means or other unknown to us, reduced to this state of insanity, those low, cunning people, the tavern-keepers, caused some form of marriage, as they allege, to be gone through between him and their daughter, with the view, no doubt, of possessing themselves of his wealth, to the loss and disgrace of his heir and high family connections. So completely had the tavern-keeper and his family got control over the poor old man, that they induced him to hire coaches and blood-horses, and dress himself out in the most grotesqne, and, at the same time, most expensive manner. They induced him also to write a letter to the recorder of Dublin and certain magistrates, a copy of which will be produced in evidence, and upon a perusal of it, it will be seen that it could only have emanated from a man stark mad. Under these circumstances, however painful it might have been to the friends of the lunatic, nothing remained but to issue this commission ; and Mr. Swingsnap, his nephew, had both the courage and humanity to come forward to rescue his uncle, as far as he could, from the wretched condition in which he was placed, and to save his property from the grasp of a gang of low swindlers, who had got the poor man into their possesion. On the whole, such clear and incontrovertible testimony will be submitted to you as will leave not a shadow of doubt of the unfortunate old man's insanity for some time previous to the alleged marriage. In finding your virdict accordingly, you will only do an act of the greatest benevolence and humanity, for you will thereby place the poor man in the hands of the best and kindest friends, who can render him every comfort and convenience that the asylum of that genuine philanthropist, Doctor Deering, can afford. I will not," he added, " say another word, but proceed to call my witnesses, and then leave the case in your hands, confidently relying that you will do your duty before God and your country."

Judith O'Shaughnessey was the first witness called, and when she came into the room she cast her eyes around with a malignant scowl, as if in search of her unfortunate master, but he was not within her view. " I want," she muttered, "to see that old villain, to show him that I can be revenged of him ; I swore I would, and I'll be as good as my oath."

"Come, my good woman," said Gripe, " calm down your feelings, and just answer this gentleman's" (pointing to Muggleton) " questions, in a voice sufficiently loud to be heard by the most distant of those gentlemen whom you see here in court." Then turning to the jury : " This poor woman has been most cruelly treated by the lunatic ; indeed, I might say, both lunatics, during the paroxysms of their insanity ; the creature feels it most acutely, as she attributed it to cruelty and caprice, and not to the real cause."

The witness was then examined at length by Muggleton, and gave satisfactory answers to all the interrogatories put to her, and left the table evidently disappointed in not having the malicious satisfaction of seeing her old master in the wretched condition to which he had been reduced, and showing him how completely she was avenged of him for slighting her affections, and breaking a promise which she alleged he had made nearly twenty years previous, to marry her if he should ever marry any woman.

Mr. Cecil, one of the magistrates to whom Old Hawk had addressed the letter in favour of Fogarty, was the next witness called. He produced a copy of the document, and desposed that the original was in the hand writing of the lunatic. He added that he had for some time entertained suspicions as to Mr. Norberry's sanity, inasmuch as he wanted him to pay a debt twice.

Swingsnap, who was anxiously watching the proceedings, said to Muggleton, Ask him did he get a receipt for the money paid."

Muggleton complied with the request, and Cecil said, " No, indeed ; I merely met him one day in the bank, and gave it to him ; he said he would send a receipt, but he did not do so."

" That will do," said Swingsnap, in an under tone.

Muggleton said, the next witness he would produce would be his inestimable and virtuous friend, Mr. Gripe. He could not undergo the ordeal of examining him ; he would let him tell his own story, and leave him in the hands of the jury.

Gripe then slowly rose from his seat, drew a large cambric handkerchief of exquisite whiteness and highly perfumed, from his pocket, applied the corner of it to his right eye—which still bore the marks of Tim's honest indignation—and ascended the witness box with a solemn air and grave deportment. When he took his place there, he drew the handkerchief from the right eye, rolled it up, rubbed it hastily two or three times across his mouth, then placed his elbow on the moulding of the jury box, his hand to his face, and, having heaved a long sigh, requested that the commissioners and the jury would bear with him for a moment until his feelings would calm down, and the painful emotions which he felt for the misfortunes of his dear friend and client would subside.

"Ah!" said Muggleton, "that manifestation of feeling does honour to humanity; there is a sight worthy of the philosopher and the Christian. Your name will be transmitted to posterity in conjunction with this case."

"Most likely," muttered Swingsnap, in an under tone.

When the worthy attorney recovered his self-composure, and was duly sworn, he entered into a long detail of the case of the lunatic, not forgetting to extol his own benevolence and philanthropy as the main spring of all his actions.

The jury seemed to evince the deepest sympathy for the witness, and the fore-- man said it was quite unnecessary to produce much further evidence after the clear and convincing testimony given by Mr. Gripe; all they wanted was to see the unfortunate lunatic, if he was in a condition to be brought before them.

Muggleton observed that in point of law such a course of proceeding was un-necessary, but the inquiry could not close without examining a medical gentleman, who would explain to them the precise nature of the disease, and the little hope that existed of his ultimate recovery.

The foreman remarked that his object in proposing an examination of the lunatic was an adjournment to the following day, but as there was another witness to be examined, it would answer his purpose and that of his brother jurors as well; and he would, with the permission of the commissioners, request a post-ponement of the proceedings.

"I was just going to state that we had gone far enough for one day," said one of the commissioners: "and as we have some other business on hand to-morrow, we shall not be able to meet until an advanced hour in the day."

"Well, then," observed several of the jurymen, all at the same moment, "it will be impossible to close the doctor's evidence to-morrow, and we must have a further adjournment."

"Of course," said one of the commissioners, "I can never sit late, and as we cannot meet till three or four o'clock, we will merely open the court pro forma, and adjourn again."

"All right, all right," exclaimed the worthy jurors, in apparent delight.

"Messrs. Commissioners, and Gentlemen of the Jury," said Muggleton, "your convenience, of course, must be consulted; but, before we break up, permit me to express the deep obligation I feel for the indulgence and courtesy extended to me in the discharge of the painful professional duty which I have been called upon to perform."

The jury and commissioners reciprocated the compliment, and the court ad-journed to three o'clock the following day.

"This is monstrous," said Swingsnap as the parties left the court. "A great portion of the property will be swallowed by this unnecessary delay and consequent expense."

"I thought you were more of a philosopher," replied Gripe; "you are going to the bar, and depend upon it you will find the chief profits of your profession shall arise from the delays of the law. If suits were to be terminated within the time that clients think they ought, it would be better to be a street knife-grinder, than a barrister or attorney. My dear young friend, although you may suffer some trivial loss or inconvenience at present, you should rejoice in the prospect of future gain, which delays similar to this may bring you."

On the following day, at the appointed hour, all the parties were punctual in their attendance, and the jury having taken their seats as on the former day, Gripe went through the process of communication with them, as already described, and then desired Doctor Deering to be called.

The doctor was not then in attendance; but after a delay of a few minutes he rushed into court, almost breathless, and apparently labouring under great excite-ment. The cause was soon explained. It appeared from his statement that the unfor-tunate Norberry had died rather suddenly that morning.

At this intelligence the countenance of Swingsnap brightened up, and he said in ªn under tone, " The cormorants are disappointed ; yes, ———them, they are ; there is an end of the proceedings."

The foreman of the jury remarked to one of his brethren, it was very lucky the news did not arrive half an hour sooner.

Gripe applied the cambric handkerchief to his eyes, and affected to shed tears copiously.

Muggleten exclaimed, " The will of heaven be done; the ways of Providence are inscrutable."

The commissioners looked somewhat amazed, declared that the proceedings had been rendered nugatory by the melancholy event that had occurred, and that the court was adjourned *sine die*.

CHAPTER VI.

SAD DISASTERS OF THE FOGARTY FAMILY.——AN HEIR BORN TO THE HOUSE OF NORBERRY.——DEATH CF KATE.——A SUIT INSTITUTED TO ESTABLISH THE RIGHT OF THE HEIR.

THE editor of these extraordinary memoirs, which are here transcribed almost without alteration in style or substance, had it suggested to him by literary friends, on whose taste and judgement he has always set a high value, to pass over the family history of Norberry, come at once to the incidents connected with the present time, and introduce to the reader in the first or second chapter, the reporter whose sketches and adventures form the great bulk of this work ; but after a careful perusal of the manuscript committed to his care, he resolved to give the whole in one connected narrative, just as he found it, that the reader, upon a comparison of the administration of the law upwards of half a century ago and at the present time, may find, notwithstanding all that is said of modern inprovements, the glories of our constitution, and the excellence of our system of jurisprudence, courts of justice have been, and still are, instruments of the grossest oppression, and " law" the origin of more tears, sorrows, and emaciating misery than " war" itself. It may be thought that the foregoing account of the proceedings under the commission of lunacy, and the details of the petty tyranny exercised towards the Fogartys, as related in the present chapter, are overdrawn pictures ; but, if we take the trouble of making minute inquiries with regard to the incidents of every day life, which are frequently occurring around us, or stop to examine scenes where many of our own acquaintances are actors, true originals will be found for pictures which at first sight may appear too highly coloured. A venerable member of the profession of solicitor, who was serving his time to Gripe when those incidents occurred, and whose honourable and upright conduct through a long life forms a strong contrast to the villainy and deceit of his late master, was, some time since, directed by the court of chancery in the progress of a celebrated suit, a branch of which is still pending, to give up documents and notes of proceedings, including the confession of Gripe (which will appear in the next chapter), and from them and memoranda made by O'Kelly, the materials for the first part of these memoirs have been taken.

But to return to the regular thread of the narrative. The unfortunate Mrs. Norberry was left, by the visit of Gripe and his party, in a state of insensibility, followed by a nervous attack from which she did not recover for nearly three weeks ; during the greater part of the time she was delirious, and repeatedly called on O'Kelly as her deliverer, and when lucid intervals occurred, she looked back upon the transactions of the last month as a troubled dream. Youth and natural buoyancy of spirits effected a recovery, which, under other circumstances, might

have been hopeless, and as soon as her removal could be effected with safety, she
was brought to the house of her parents in Dublin, presenting a melancholy contrast to the condition in which she left it little more than a month previous. The
only account with regard to her ill-fated husband that reached her, was, that his
friends believed him to be mad, and had him taken into custody ; but where he was
or in what way he left his affairs, she knew nothing, and the state of painful anxiety
to which she and her parents, who had built up all their hopes of future aggrandise-

THE DUEL BETWEEN GRIPE AND SWINGSNAP.

ment upon an alliance with the wealthy Norberry, had been reduced, rendered
them totally unfit to pursue their usual avocations, and their house soon assumed
the appearance of a concern going to decay.

The Cavanaghs, on the other side of the way, who would not on the day of
Kate's marriage gratify Mrs. Fogarty by looking at the splendid equipage as it
drove from the door of the " Ram," were perpetually at their windows talking so
loudly about Kate and her great match, that they could be heard by Mrs. Fogarty

No. 8,

whenever she ventured to go so far as the street door of her own house. The poor woman's pride was sadly humbled, by daily beholding the melancholy condition of her beautiful and blooming daughter, who, were it not for the precipitancy with which she had been forced into a marriage with Norberry, might have been allied to the brave O'Kelly, the object of her affections, and have the honour of being the wife of an officer in the British army.

These reflections were almost too much for Mrs. Fogarty to bear, and she was from day to day in a state bordering on insanity. She knew nothing of the nature of the proceedings that had been adopted against Old Hawk, and she fancied, perhaps truly, that law could not give her any redress. She saw her daughter's hopes blighted, her constitution impaired, and a weight of sorrow preying upon her heart, which was increased by the prospect of becoming a mother.

Mrs. Cavanagh, who was one of the Kinshelas of Catherlogh, and possessed a genuine Irish heart, having heard all the particulars of the disasters that had befallen the Fogartys, and the condition that Kate was in, was deeply affected. She warned her daughters never to be seen at the windows again, whilst talking over the condition of their unfortunate neighbours, and asserted it was their duty to commiserate and sympathise with them in their sorrows, and although they had not been on good terms for some time, she determined to pay them a visit, and be good friends with them for the future. Accordingly on the following morning she fulfilled her promise. Mrs. Fogarty, who, setting aside her vanity and a perpetual *penchant* to make herself appear superior to others, was of a generous disposition, and ever ready to reciprocate kindness, was almost dumb with surprise when she saw her neighbour, to whom she had not spoken for many years, enter her house. She thought at first that the visit was made by way of exultation over the misfortunes that had befallen her; but the supposition was removed when she saw Mrs. Cavanagh burst into tears, and heard her exclaim, " My dear Mrs. Fogarty, my heart would not allow me to be unfriendly with you, when I found that sorrow and trouble had come over you. I felt as if one of my own children was at the point of death when I saw your beautiful daughter the other day so thin and wasted away, that I would not have known her had I met her in a strange place."

Mrs. Fogarty was completely overpowered by such a manifestation of noble sentiment and generous feeling on the part of this good woman, and she embraced her with the warmest affection, and gave vent to her feelings in a copious flood of tears.

" I knew," said Mrs. Cavanagh, " that I could never be mistaken as to your real character, and it is my fault more than your's that there has not been that friendly intercourse between us which ought always to subsist between near neighbours."

" Arrah, a cushla," said Mrs. Fogarty, " the fault was mine, and now I feel what a bad part I acted, and I am ashamed of myself. I have got a *scallah chree* (a scalded heart), and it is great ease to me to have your friendship. Come down, Kate; come down till you welcome our kind fried, Mrs. Cavanagh."

Kate presently appeared, and the three ladies retired to a private room to talk over the strange vicissitudes that had occured within so brief a period.

Mrs. Cavanagh, who was a woman infinitely superior to her neighbours in information and a knowledge of the world, having been educated by a wealthy relation in Dublin, after listening to a minute detail of the particulars of Kate's marriage, and the detention of old Norberry as a lunatic, advised the Fogartys to put the case into the hands of able lawyers, who could not fail to bring it to a successful issue.

The advice and sympathy thus given to Kate and her mother imparted a degree of comfort to them which they had not felt since the unhappy marriage took place, and the party separated that night with the understanding that an attorney should be sent for, with directions to be there on the following morning, to whom the whole matter would be submitted. It was agreed, too, that Mrs. Cavanagh should be present at the interview with the man of law.

Mr. Wormwood, of Peter-street, one of the most expert practitioners in a general way that Dublin could then boast of, was accordingly apprised on that night that his presence would be required the next morning at the Ram Hotel, where business of great importance was to be submitted to him.

Wormwood was a man who paid attention to a suit just proportioned to the weight of his client's purse, or the remuneration contingent upon a certainty of success. He had been in early life an attorney's clerk and process-server, and was intimately acquainted with all the low practices of the profession, and thoroughly understood the value of a shilling, so that he had not only contrived to scrape some money together, but had got a reputation amongst the people of being a man of great cleverness, and very lucky in the prosecution of any suit which he might undertake, and it was this opinion of him that induced his selection as the law agent of the Fogartys upon the present important occasion.

When the message requiring his attendance at the "Ram" arrived, he happened to be in consultation with the friends of a merchant's clerk, who was accused of embezzling a large sum of his master's money, and whose trial was to take place on the following day. When he received the note which had been written by Kate, he read it aloud to his clients.

"There," said he, "you see the high esteem in which I am held, and the pressure of business that is upon me, and still you higgle about a fee. I am wanted to-morrow morning by a wealthy hotel keeper in the city to take up a case where there are upwards of fifty thousand pounds at stake, but still I would not desert any prior engagement I might have on hand, provided the parties deal fairly with me."

"Oh!" said the brother of the accused, "not another word; you must have whatever you require, sooner than lose your services."

"Be easy for a moment," rejoined Wormwood, "you know I would scorn to drive a hard bargain, and that I would as soon conduct your case gratis, as if I got a hundred guineas, if I thought you had not the means to pay me; but I know you have the money amongst you that was alleged to have been embezzled, and I am of course entitled to a thumping fee.

"I said you should get whatever you demanded; I have the money here."

"Very well," said Wormwood, eyeing a bag of guineas which the speaker had in his hand, and then turning round to the messenger who brought him Mrs. Norberry's note, said, "tell your mistress I shall be with her the day after to-morrow, although I am to receive a fee of twenty guineas from another party in case I attend to their business, but I feel interested in the affair about which your mistress has written to me, and I shall attend to it in preference to any other. I would attend to-morrow but I am in the middle of a criminal prosecution, where the life and liberty of my client are at stake, and once I take up the defence of any one I never relinquish it till I bring the proceedings to a close, even though my clients could not afford to pay me a shilling, and that other parties wanting me might give me a thousand guineas. Tell your mistress that; tell Fogarty of the 'Ram,' who often supplied me with post-horses when going to the country, what I have stated to you, and I am sure he will appreciate the purity of my motives. Away with you—tell all I have stated, and here is a shilling for yourself."

The messenger of Mrs. Fogarty brought to her, without the slightest loss in the carriage, a full, true and particular account of all that Wormwood had said, and added, by way of personal opinion,—

"Ah, that's a real gintleman, any one who would look at him must admit that he was accustomed to gentility—a real, real gintleman."

Kate and her mother was by no means displeased to hear the favourable account of Wormwood given by the servant, who concealed the fact of having received the gratuity, which no doubt formed the basis upon which the good opinion so freely pronounced had been founded.

On the following morning, whilst the Fogarty family were mournfully sitting at breakfast in a little room off the bar, the two watchmen already alluded to, accompanied by a person apparently in a higher station, entered the tap-room, and demanded, in an imperative tone, that the person who had the license for that house should immediately appear. Fogarty laid down his cup of tea, and went out to meet his new visitors.

"Ho! Mr. Fogarty," said the person who accompanied the watchmen, " you have a license for this house?"

"Yes, your honour, I have."

"Well, then, we are come to tell you that your business as an innkeeper is at an end, and that we have a warrant for your arrest, as a suborner of crime, and an accessary after the fact of most of the murders and outrages committed in Tipperary."

"God protect me!" said Fogarty, "what have I done? I am as innocent as a child."

"None of your palavering," said one o the watchmen; "you have not your old friend Norberry to bamboozle the magistrates. D—— me but it was a nice business indeed, to be humbugged by an old madman. The recorder and magistrates will never forgive themselves for being so taken in; but it is all for the better. We have got fresh evidence since we were here before, so that there was 'luck in leisure, and pleasure in waiting for it.' You now see we are here again."

"What in the name of mercy is all this about?" said Mrs. Fogarty; "are our misfortunes never to end? What have we done, that we are to be treated this way; my poor husband arrested, and our house shut up?"

"I scorns to hold up any altereation with a faymale" said the speaker, who had been just deploring the simplicity of the magistrates. "Our business is short and sweet, and with your leave, ma'am, we will try a drop of your brandy." So stepping into the bar, he helped himself and his comrade, and two or three others of the fraternity, who had, by this time, arrived upon speculation, or to give their assistance in conveying Fogarty to Newgate, in case any resistance should be made.

There was then an active search made through the whole house, on pretence of looking for papers connected with the movement of the Whiteboys in Munster, which at the time assumed a very formidable appearance, but there was noh g found to show that poor Fogarty had any communication with them. This, however, was of no avail; informations had been sworn against him on the ground that he aided and abetted in the escape of a notorious criminal from Tipperary, for whose apprehension there was a large reward, but who was supposed to have got off to America disguised in female apparel.

The fate of this unhappy family seemed to be sealed. Fogarty was brought off to Newgate by his old friends the watchmen and their assistants, who told him on the way that they were about to make good their promise of hunting him out of Dublin. It might have satisfied them at first to send him back to Tipperary amongst the rebels; but at present they were bound to tell him in a friendly way, that the magistrates would not be satisfied till they sent him over the herring-brook; but, as he would be sure to meet plenty of his friends in Botany Bay, he would be more at home there than any place else he could be sent to, and that ought to be a consolation to his mind.

Fortunately for poor Kate, she was brought the evening before by the kind-hearted Mrs. Cavanagh to a cottage which she had in the neighbourhood of Rath-farnham, and was thus saved the pain of being present at the fresh misfortune which had befallen the family.

After Fogarty was transmitted to Newgate, the Ram Hotel was shut up, and the strange vicissitudes which had so recently occurred, and the mystery that hung over everything lately connected with the Fogartys, was the perpetual theme of conversation in the neighbourhood.

Mrs. Fogarty would have been wholly unable to support those fresh trials, were it not for the advice and sympathy of Mrs. Cavanagh, who arranged that Kate should be kept in the country, in ignorance of what had happened until measures could be taken to redress the evils which had befallen them, and, above all, obtain her father's release from prison.

Mr. Wormwood was punctual in his attendance at the appointed, time, but was a good deal surprised to find the "Ram" shut up, Fogarty in Newgate, and his unfortunate wife in a state of distraction bodering on despair.

"Ho! ho!" said he, "this is a bad business; who is to be my client in the matter? the owner of this house is in Newgate, and most probably may be transported, and if I take up the business at all I must of course be paid beforehand."

Mrs. Cavanagh was sent for to be present at the interview between the worthy attorney and Mrs. Fogarty, and when he head all the facts circumstantially related, and that he found so wealthy a subject in the case as old Norberry, his little eyes began to glisten at the prospect of a long chancery suit, in which there would be ample funds to pay costs as it proceeded. Mrs. Norberry would soon be a mother, and let the lunacy proceedings end as they might, the heir would be entitled to the property; then all that was wanted was some money in hand, to pay the costs out of pocket, it being an invariable rule with him never to undertake any suit without obtaining funds from some quarter to that amount at least.

"Well," said he, when he' had fully heard the case, "all that's wanted now is some money, without which I cannot stir a peg; but from what I hear, there can be no doubt that I will secure the property for your daughter and her child; and as her unfortunate husband is mad, and that she never had any liking for him, he may as well be left where ever he is."

"Oh!" said Mrs. Fogarty, " try in the first place if you could get my unfortunate husband out of gaol; for until we have him out it will be impossible to get any money for the purposes of the suit."

"In that case," replied Wormwood, " we must see what can be done." He accordingly went that day, obtanied a copy of his committal, and made some preparations for defending him at the commission of Oyer and Terminer, which was to take place within the following week. In the meantime, Mrs. Fogarty supplied him with the money necessary for that occasion, and Fogarty promised as soon as he got out to raise funds necessary for going on with the suit to establish the rights of his daughter.

The commission sat on the appointed day, the lord chief justice of the King's Bench, and Mr. Justice Patterson presided, and, to the joy and astonishment of Fogarty, he was discharged by proclamation. But the opening of his house for business was quite another affair. Such permission wholly rested with the recorder and magistrates, and all attempts to procure a restoration of his license were ineffectual. He accordingly came to the resolution to sell his house and furniture to raise money to carry on the suit, and through the agency of Wormwood he was not long effecting his purpose.

Funds being thus obtained, the first step taken by the worthy attorney was to call on Gripe, whom he discovered to be the solicitor in the lunacy proceedings. He was astonished beyond bounds when he heard old Norbery had died in the mad house a few days previous, and that consequently there was no finding of the jury in the case. Gripe also assured him that no legal marriage, indeed he believed no marriage at all had taken place between him and Fogarty's daughter, and the whole was a fabrication—a scheme to get possession of the unfortunate madman's property.

Wormwood was considerably nonplussed by this intelligence, and returned to poor Fogarty to communicate what he had heard, but he consoled himself that he had already obtained money more than sufficient to pay him for any trouble he had been at.

The Fogartys heard this new disaster with great surprise, but they were latterly so accustomed to accumulated misfortunes, that their hearts were hardened, and new sorrows could affect them little. When Mrs. Fogarty heard it alleged that her daughter was not married, she could not restrain her ingidnation: " Not married!" she exclaimed; " she was not only married in St. Patrick's church, but afterwards married in our own house by the great Father O'Leary, who, I am proud to say, is her own cousin."

"Hold your tongue, you stupid woman," said Wormwood; "if you want to get O'Leary hanged or transported, you will speak about his having married your daughter to old Norberry; but if a marriage took place at Patrick's church all is right. and I will go at once and get a certificate, which will set the matter at rest."

The news of old Norberry's death was communicated to Kate by the kind and considerate Mrs. Cavanagh. She received the intelligence with composure; she felt that her health was so much impaired that there was little probability of her surviving the event which was shortly to occur. All her hopes of happiness were blighted, and she regarded those new strokes of misfortune with perfect resignation and fortitude.

Wormwood proceeded to obtain the marriage certificate, but by some unacountable fatality there was no record of the event to be found; and when the curate who performed the ceremony was applied to, he stated most truly that he had not any distinct recollection of the transaction. He remembered that about the time alleged to, he had married some persons between whom a great disparity of years existed, but he could not charge his memory further with the matter: he would not know any one of the parties if they were before him. It was, however, the business of the clerk to enter all marriages, and he, of course, had entered the one in question.

A visit to the clerk was attended with a little success. He remembered a very old gentleman and a young lady coming to be married, but as soon the parties had entered the church, the intended bride began to shy at the matter, when she looked the old fellow straight in the face. She fainted, or pretended to faint, and was carried out to the carriage, and never saw her since. That was his recollection of the transaction. Sure if a marriage did take place, he added, it would be down there in black and white, and it would be all for his profit, as he would be paid his fee for the certificate.

Wormwood returned to his unfortunate clients wholly at a loss with regard to what course of proceeding he should adopt. He did not wish to relinquish a cause where ultimately there would be ample funds to meet all expenses, and where there could hardly be a doubt that he would establish the right of Mrs. Norberry; for although there was no record of the marriage in the parish books, there were two witnesses who happened to be in St. Patrick's church when the marriage was celebrated, and who were ready to depose to the fact. With regard to the performance of the ceremony by Dr. O'Leary, although there was indisputable evidence of it, it could not be legally relied on.

In this state of perplexity, Wormwood postponed proceeding in the matter until after the confinement of Mrs Norberry.

In the meantime ruin had overtaken the poor Fogartys: their little substance was completely wasted; their son, a fine young lad, emigrated to America; Kate's sister, a sweet little girl, was taken into the family of Mrs. Cavanagh, and treated as one of her own children.

Mrs. Norberry gave birth to a son, which event she survived but a few hours. This was an additional misfortune to her parents, which they did not long survive. The poor father was attacked with paralysis and general debility, and in three months after the death of his daughter, he was interred in her grave in the hospital fields. His wife survived him but a few weeks, and was laid in the same tomb with her husband and child.

Mrs. Cavanagh, whose kindness and attention helped to console the last sad hours of the unfortunate Fogartys, had a nurse provided for the child of Kate, and every necessary attention paid to it.

In the meantime Wormwood called again upon Gripe, to inform him that unless a compromise was entered into, or some arrangement made, he would be obliged to file a bill in the name of the infant child of Mrs. Norberry to set aside all the proceedings that had taken place with regard to old Norberry, and secure the property for the real heir.

The intelligence of an heir being in question, which was new to Gripe, seemed to startle him considerably, and he exclaimed that such a circumstance was an insurmountable bar to any settlement or compromise; a legal marriage had taken place, or it had not; if it had, it was not in the power of any agent to make any settlements that would bind the minor; if it had not, which in point of fact was the case, no offer of compromise could be entertained for a moment.

Wormwood found there was nothing left but to commence hostilities forthwith, and in order to supply himself with additional funds beyond what he had received from Fogarty whilst living, he took out letters of administration to the remnant of property he left behind him, and, thus furnished with means, he filed his bill in the name of the infant child of poor Kate. It is unnecessary to say that he was brought by Gripe through the intricate paths and perplexing byways that lead to the temple of justice in that happy land, and that he was met at every turn by all the barriers which some thousands of ponderous volumes, all contradictory of each other, could present. There were depositions on both sides. which ran to one thousand sheets ; then there were answers, replications, demurrers, rejoinders, rebutters, and sub-rebutters, founded either upon some flaw discovered in the pleadings, or fresh evidence, so that it would seem as if all the quibbles and quirks of the law had been completely exhausted before the merits of the case had been touched upon. Thus matters went on for upwards of two years, Gripe still drawing largely upon Swingsnap, who was administrator of the property of Old Hawk. for funds to prosecute the suit, when an event was announced which changed the whole aspect of affairs as regarded all parties concerned.

The child of Kate had been sent to nurse in the county Wicklow, and between the affectionate attentions of Mrs. Cavanagh, and those bestowed by Wormwood, from motives of a verry different character, was well taken care of, and had become a most promising boy. The woman in whose care he was, evinced the greatest fondness for him, and having occasion to go to the county Wexford, she took the child with her, and had been there only a week or two when she wrote to Mrs. Cavanagh, stating that poor little Robert had suddenly died of quinsey, notwithstanding the attention of two of the most eminent doctors in that part of the country. This news was received by Wormwood with the utmost dismay. When the letter arrived which conveyed it, he mounted his horse and rode night and day till he reached Wexford. He found the nurse in apparent sorrow for the loss of her dear boy, as he called him, and a conference with the medical men left no doubt whatever on his mind that the child had died from natural causes. What was to be done ? The suit was abated after an outlay of several hundred pounds of his own, besides whatever little property poor Fogarty left. He cursed the fates, got into convulsions from rage, not so much from the loss he had sustained as the triumph thus given to Gripe, who had, throughout the whole proceedings, harrassed and annoyed him by every means which the dark windings of the law would permit. He put his wits to work, and bethought of buying the nurse over to secresy about the matter, and as it would be very easy to obtain a child about the same age, the suit might still be carried on, until his costs would be secured by a decree. He suggested the matter to the nurse, who, to his astonishment, peremptorily refused to be a party to any such arrangement. She had already communicated the news to her friends in Dublin, she would of course make no secret of it, and such an attempt would only lead to exposure and disgrace. Wormwood felt the force of this reasoning, and returned to Dublin in a state of distraction at his misfortune. On his arrival he was surprised to find the death of the heir of Norberry inserted in the *Hibernian Magazine, Dublin Evening Post, and Freeman's Journal.* Who could have been the author of these paragraphs ? The thing was startling and mysterious. Could Gripe have been at work to put the child out of the way or cause its death? There was nothing infamous and diabolical that his malice could not suggest, and his skill accomplish, On the whole, Wormwood concluded that a short cut had been taken to put an end to the suit, and determined that the circumstances attending the death of young Norberry should be further investigated. He proceeded again to Wexford, and had a notice served on the coroner to exhume the deceased child, and hold an inquest, in order to ascertain, without any doubt whatever, the cause of its death. In the meantime he set about procuring witnessess, and everything was ready for inquiry, when it was ascertained that the nurse had returned to Dublin on the day that Wormwood arrived in Wexford. She was of course the most material witness, but the coroner decided upon going on without her; all he wanted was the medical men; for to swear to the identity of the child in its present state, he thought [impossible. The worthy functionary was brother-in-law to one of the doctors and a relation to the other, and although not displeased at discharging a duty which would bring his medical friends a guinea or two each, yet he felt that their honour and integrity were in some degree impeached by doubting for a moment that the death had occurred in the way described by them.

Wormwood prayed for an adjournment, till the nurse would be brought back from Dublin, and the attendance of some other witnessess procured whose evidence he deemed necessary for a full and satisfactory investigation.

"You are not come here to teach me my business, I presume, Mr. Attorney from Dublin," said the coroner, with an air of dignity.

"By no means," replied Wormwood, " but I have come here to assist in eliciting the truth in a case which appears to me me to wear a very suspicious aspect. Your worship cannot go on without witnesses."

" To elicit truth is my object always ; and I can tell you, Mr. Attorney, when I go in pursuit of it, I shall not call at your ffice in Dublin. As to witnesses I see many here waiting to be examined, who were served at your desire with my summons to attend. You have been beating up for testimony since you came to Wexford, and now indeed you call for an adjournment. You ought to know sir, that this is not an inquiry at your suit ; it is one on the part of our sovereign lord, the king, to ascertain when, where, how, and in what manner the deceased—barony constable, what is the name of the individual now lying dead then and there ?"

Constable—"Oh ! it's only a little child, your worship ; I believe no one knows its name."

The coroner proceeded—

" I tell you sir, that this is an inquiry on the part of our sovereign lord the king, who has empowered me, by my precept, to call together twelve or more loyal subjects—good men and true—to ascertain when, where, how, and in what manner, an individual—name unknown—now lying dead in the parish of Oilgate, barony of Scaravage, town land of Inchpruck, county of Wexford, and kingdom of Ireland, came by his death. This is my duty, sir, and I am sure after being one-and-twenty years in the high judicial station I have the honour to fill, I know how to discharge it. Take the book, Mr. Juror, and hearken to your oath. Constables, keep silence out there, and don't be talking about search warrants for stolen fowl whilst I am performing the high duty of administering the juror's oath. You shall well and truly try, and diligently inquire, when, where, how, and in what manner— G—— d—— it, will you stop your noise outside there, whilst I am administering the juror's oath ; this is no place to be talking about tresspass of goats and pounding of cattle ; it is one thing to sit as a magistrate, and another as a coroner ; when this inquest is over, you can go on with these cases. But I can tell you, beforehand, that the fowl never was stolen. I dined at Squire Gulliver's yesterday, and eat my share of a fine fat turkey that was one of what Devereux said was stole from him ; his wife made a present of them to the landlord, and was then afraid to tell her husband. That's the upshot of that story. Silence there. Come, sir, hearken to your oath. You shall well and truly try, and diligently inquire."

A constable here cried out—

" There's a young woman, your worship, with a child in her arms, wanting to force into the court."

" Come, come, I must exercise my authority, and commit any one who shal for the future attempt to disturb the proceedings."

Mr. Wormwood here remarked that as his worship seemed to act in the double and, he should add, inconsistent capacity, of coroner and magistrate, he might, with the less inconvenience to himself, adjourn the inquest as soon as he had

worn the jury, and attended to his magisterial duties, which seemed to be very ressing.

" What's this I hear?" said his worship, becoming fiercely indignant, " incon-iistent in my conduct in acting as magistrate and coroner, eh ! Is that what you say, Mr. Attorney from Dublin ? I was a magistrate when I was appointed coroner, and I have acted as one ever since without being questioned ; the people all come to me, and I settle their disputes without having recourse to such nen as you are. I keep them out of law. My father had a good estate ; he was

No. 9.

a magistrate also, and he never let a tenant stop a day on it who brought an action against another tenant; he used to settle all disputes. I copy so far after him, and never let any one go to law that I can prevent. What are magistrates for but to decide everything? As to your courts in Dublin, I was never in them, and I hope I never will; I'd as soon go in amongst a den of thieves. Having, said so much, sir, I now tell you to keep yourself quiet. Just keep your toe in your pump or I'll commit you while you'dbe saying amen. I know my duty and my power; the lord lieutenant dare not move me from my office. Come, now, be silent every mother's son of you."

"I presume," said Wormwood, "that your office continues *dum se bene gesserit.*"

"Continues what? Should continue dumb, and what else do you say? Oh! I see that a friendly caution is of no use to you; I should commit you at once, but I'll be content to put you out of court. Constables, show that Dublin jackeen the colour of the walls outside."

"I have come here to assist professionally in this investigation, and I claim my right to be present; if I have done anything to offend your worship, I can only say I did not intend it; but you insulted me grossly."

"There is nothing ill said but what is ill taken, and you ought to be greatly obliged to me for not sending you to gaol; but I see, after all, you are a bad lawyer, you have no right to be professionally here; we dont want your assistance, except you wish to be sworn as a witness, and if you do you shall be called in. Constables, put him outside, and put his name on the list of witnesses if he wishes to be examined."

The order of the worthy coroner was forthwith obeyed, and as Wormwood left the house he declared he would report the case to the lord chancellor.

"Is it the chancellor he's threatening me with?" said his worship. "His lordship may go hang himself any day he likes for all I care, and provided he would do so in the county of Wexford, the sooner the better."

After two or three other interruptions, this celebrated functionary swore the jury, and proceeded to examine the witnesses.

The woman at whose house the nurse and child lodged was first examined. She deposed that they came there a few weeks previous; the nurse told her the child's name was Norberry, and that it was heir to a great fortune, about which a law-suit was going on; it was ailing when it came there, and seemed to get worse every day, although every care and attention was paid to it; the nurse had plenty of money, and doctors Leech and Flam were called in to attend it; they would, of course, be able to tell what ailed it."

"Clear and conclusive evidence," said the coroner. "The depositions must be read over to that Dublin prig, just to show him how we do business here."

The two doctors, who were men of skill and good practice in that part of the country, were examined. They deposed that they had been called in to attend a sick child, as described by the last witness, and found it affected by water on the brain; they deemed the case incurable from the first, but the child would have lived much longer had it not been attacked with quinsey; it survived but a few days under the double complaint, they had made a post mortem examination, which fully bore out the truth of their evidence, the nurse represented the child to be an orphan named Robert Norberry, who would be entitled to a very large fortune, and they had no reason to doubt what she stated."

Wormwood was then called in, the depositions read over to him and being asked if he had any evidence to give, he seemed sadly puzzled what to think, and replied in the negative.

"This," said the coroner, "is the great case about which this Dublin attorney has been making so much noise in the country since he came here; and all I know is, that if we had many like him, who would cause an inquest to be held upon every brat that died in the country with quinsey, small-pox, or any other complaint, it would be good times for me. There is no doubt whatever, but I approve highly of circumspection and watchfulness w ith regard to sudden deaths; and every good subject of the king should be aiding and abetting their discovery, with a view, in the first place, to uphold the dignity of the ancient and high office of coroner, and in the next place to bring guilty parties to justice where deaths take place from lawless violence; but in the present case no such motive actuated this Dublin attorney."

Here the foreman of the jury, to whom this extraordinary address was directed, bowed assent, and two or three of his brethren turned to him, and said in a tone loud enough to be heard by all present, "He has, with his usual ability, taken the attorney's measure; he is stating the real facts."

Thus encouraged, the worshipful functionary proceeded—"Yes, gentlmen, we have been called here by an attorney to hold this inquiry, not with a view to sustain the laws, but either to gratify a spirit of revenge against some party not before us now, or probably to possess himself of whatever propertythe deceased might ultimately become entitled to. We, of course, cannot exactly tell what his motives were, but, from his conduct in court to-day you may fairly judge if I be much mistaken."

Here the foreman again bowed assent, and was supported by the approving voices of his brother jurors, whilst unfortunate Wormwood was writhing with rage, which was suppressed by the presence of half a dozen yeomen, armed with old Queen Anne muskets, and as many more barony constables, all ready to convey any delinquent to prison who might disturb the court whilst his worship was delivering his charge. There seemed to be that understanding between the coroner, the constables, the doctors, and the jury, which is generally the result of an identity of interests. The constables were the heralds who conveyed the pleasing intelligence of violent or accidental deaths, and were always welcomed with delight, and treated to the best fare the coroner's house could afford. The doctors shared their fees with his worship, and often certified that persons were poisoned who died from the effects of intoxication. (That, however, would be no great violation of truth.) This gave employment to the barony constables, who were then paid whilst on duty, to search for the supposed criminals, and whilst thus engaged they generally stumbled upon another case of sudden death, which put his worship in motion again and as it was desirable that he should in all cases be able to obtain juries with the least possible delay, he frequently ordered dinner and potteen for them at the next public house, so that there was some profit as well as honour connected with their office. The union of sentiment that excited between all these parties was therefore admirable, and might serve as a model for a form of government where every man would have an interest in upholding the state, and preserving the institutions of the country from the changes which frequently arise from divisions amongst the people. Such was the popularity of the worthy functionary, that if the government attempted to remove him, most probably the yeomen would have thrown down their arms, the barony constables become Whiteboys, and the independent voters of the country refused to vote for the friends or connections of any one who had anything to say in the transaction. His worship was therefore perfectly secure in his place, no matter what complaints might be made against him, and he laughed to scorn the idle threat of Wormwood, who had no one present to bear testimony for him.

The jury brought in a verdict that the child died from natural causes, and the attorney returned to Dublin hardly able to bear up against the weight of sorrow, disappointment, and vexation, which preyed upon him. He saw that there was an end of the suit, and that the golden harvest which he had expected to reap had been blighted. On his arrival in town, he found a notice before him, to stay proceedings, as the suit had been abated, and calling upon him to pay a considerable sum in the shape of costs, on account of some laches of which he had been guilty, and which arose from his attention to the inquest in the country, and his efforts to discover that some trick had been played with regard to the death of the heir. A complication of troubles and disappointments, at the moment when he fancied he was about to bring the suit to a successful issue, had driven him almost to despair, and he was only consoled by recollecting that he had another suit in hand that success, and the total ruin of an old and inveterate enemy were placed beyond the possibility of a doubt. As those salutary reflections crossed his mind, he exclaime " Can anything be so exquisite as to witness the defeat, the ruin, the prostratiod, the sorrow, the misery of an envenomed, malignant, and once dangerous foe ? No; there are better days in store for me, and I will live to enjoy them. If I have been defeated by the villain Gripe, I have defeated a still greater villain if it be possible that one could be found. I never knew Gripe, except by name, until the present suit was instituted, and, after all he has done nothing—has taken no advantage but that which the law sanctions ; and if he has been able to bribe the nurse to either cause the death of the heir, or put him out of the way, and substitute another in his place without detection, it only proved his skill; it was what a man of business and of the world ought to have done. It was all fair, exceedingly fair, and I have got a lesson by which I may profit. I admire you, Gripe; I admire you exceedingly ; and I would be a great fool to feel perpetual discontent because you defeated me, particularly when so much enjoyment awaits me." After thus soliloquizing, Wormwood walked down stairs to his office, gave an order to his clerk to attend to the taxation of the costs which Gripe claimed in the cause of Norberry, a lunatic, and directed that the proceedings in the other cause where his triumph was certain, should not be delayed a moment.

"Issue," said he, " at once an attachment for contempt, for not putting in an answer to my supplemental bill, although I know the ruined wretch has not in the world what would pay for the parchment upon which it must be engrossed. No matter, let him be arrested, and a receiver placed over his property ; he shall end his life in a gaol."

So saying, Wormwood sat down to his business, endeavouring to forget the unfortunate result of the Norberry suit, and the contumelious treatment he received at the hands of the Wexford coroner. It was no doubt a trial sufficient to test the patience of any attorney, and his enduring powers were stretched still further when his clerk brought him back word that Gripe had obtained a taxation behind his back, with an immediate order for the payment of the costs in question.

Upon this news being conveyed to him, he raved, swore, foamed at the mouth, and exclaimed that he would be well satisfied to suffer eternal punishment if he could have revenge on Gripe. He could, however, get the taxation overhauled, but as he had eventually to pay costs, a few shillings or a few pounds were of no great consequence, and if he was to go over the business again it would only remind him of his defeat in the Norberry suit; so he made up his mind to pay the demand and have done with Gripe. He, however, vowed vengeance, and he was often heard to declare that he had never determined upon doing harm to any individual that he was not able to accomplish his purpose, or gratify his revenge in some way or other. He sat down, and wrote at considerable length in his memorandum-book, a full account of his transactions with Gripe, and the bad treatment he had received from the Wexford functionary, and recorded a vow at the bottom of his statement, that he would be revenge of both, although he believed the latter reached with difficulty. At the same time there was no knowing what might turn up, and he would keep him on his list, so that his memory might be refreshed whenever an opportunity should occur. Notwithstanding the result of the inquests, he was by no means satisfied that the heir had not been put out of the way, and his suspicions upon this head were strengthened by the fruitless attempts he had made to discover where the nurse was when he came back to Dublin ; but under the circumstances it was impossible that he could do anything to extricate himself from the difficulty in which he was involved, so there was nothing left for the present but to sit down and chew the bitter cud of disappointment.

CHAPTER VII.

FUNERAL OF OLD HAWK—A DUEL—THE REVENGE OF WORMWOOD GRATIFIED.

AFTER the termination of the proceedings under the commissioners of lunacy in the manner already stated, Gripe and his client walked together to the office of the former in St. Andrew Street. "This is a highly satisfactory termination of the proceedings," said Swingsnap, as they went along; "our most sanguine expectations could hardly have anticipated such a result as this; but do you think that the tongues of scandal can catch hold of anything? You know I am tenacious of my fame, as I am about to be called to the bar, and also to a seat in the Irish house."

"You need not have the smallest apprehensions about the matter," said Gripe; "everything has been done with such care and circumspection, that the tongue of calumny cannot utter a suspicion with regard to our proceedings. The commission was legally issued, commissioners presided, and a jury regularly empannelled; and then as to the treatment in the asylum, we are not accountable for that. Doctor Deering bears a high character; he visits at the castle; has many of the aristocracy for his patients, and no one can ever imagine that he treated the lunatic in any other way than that which the nature of his complaint warranted. Indeed, I am quite certain of that fact myself; but now that the old fellow is gone, and has left all his wealth behind him, he must be interred with some pomp and solemnity. A few pounds additional laid out on his funeral may stifle any ill-natured remarks, even if busy people were inclined to make them."

"I agree with you," said the client, "and in this, as well as in legal matters, I will wholly submit to your judgment and discretion. I think we must have a respectable funeral."

"A magnificent funeral," added Gripe. "I will go now and give directions to Mr. Muffle, the undertaker, to do the thing in style; he is a friend of mine, and has already buried thirty or forty of my richest clients; and as in the present case, I really know not whether I profited more by their death than if they had lived longer. Muffle is an excellent fellow, and he shall have the funeral of your uncle. You and I shall attend as chief mourners, the doctor shall occupy the second carriage, and it might be well if we were to have Muggleten there too."

"Yes," said Swingsnap; "we shall all then be going home with our work, like the tailors."

"Oh! my young friend," rejoined Gripe, "you have reason to be facetious; but there is a time for all things, and reserve your jokes for another occasion; be guided by your legal adviser and preceptor."

"Very well," said the client, with a serious air, "you are my mentor, and I trust I shall prove myself a disciple worthy of such a master; but tell me seriously how it will be about the money the doctor got for the support of the lunatic? Surely he is not entitled to keep it, as the death occurred so soon."

"I fear," replied Gripe, "that this perpetual penchant you have to be looking after trifles—this penny wise and pound foolish system—will only lead to troubles and difficulties that you do not foresee. The thing could never have been managed without the doctor, and we are very safe if he cries 'quits' as the matter stands."

Swingsnap, although far from being satisfied, was silent, and the rebuke which he received prevented him from making any inquiry then about the bags of gold which had been deposited in the strong box of Gripe a few weeks previously.

The gentlemen separated for the evening—Gripe to give instruction to Muffle to convey the remains of the old Norberry to his last home in splendour, and Swingsap, who inherited the love of money peculiar to his family, to consider how he could best rescue the property of his deceased relative from the fangs of the avaricious and crafty attorney.

Muffle, who owed Gripe a bill of costs, was directed by him to spare no expense and when the job was finished to send him in his bill with a receipt to it, credit for which would be given in the account for costs. A promise was made at the same time by the worthy attorney that he would soon put other good jobs in the way of the undertaker.

The funeral was conducted upon a very respectable scale, and, on the second morning following, the remains of old Norberry were conveyed from the asylum, followed by a long line of carriages, three-fourths of which were empty, and deposited in the vaults underneath the church of St. Patrick, where a handsome monument was erected inside the building, to mark the spot where they lay.

In a few weeks after the funeral, Gripe was directed by his young client to call in the amount of the various bonds, mortgages, money in the funds, and other securities. Whilst preparations were being made for the performance of this agreeable duty, prsceedings were, as already stated, commenced by Wormwood, with the view to establish the right of Old Hawk's child to the property.

Swingsnap, who thought he had the immense wealth of his uncle nearly seeure in his pocket, heard the intelligence with dismay. Notices were served upon all parties having property in their hands belonging to the late Mr. Norberry, or owing him money, directing that they should not part with or pay away the same until a receiver in the cause would be appointed, or a decree of the court made, commanding them to do so. Amongst others, a notice to this effect was served upon Gripe, which he at once put into the hands of his client, declaring that such was always his respect for the law, that not even in the smallest particular would be violate it, and he should therefore keep whatever money he had belonging to the deceased sealed up until an order with regard to it would be made.

Swingsnap, who had on the morning of the day upon which he had received this intelligence, been called to the bar, and designated for shortness Counsellor Swing, made his first *ex parte* motion in his own cause, and was most favourably heard by the court. His application was that a sum of money should be ordered to be placed to the credit of the cause, to be applicable to the payment of costs incurred in resisting a most unfounded claim to the property, which had been set up by parties who induced a litigious attorney to act for them in the matter. A conditional order was granted, but when Wormwood came to show cause against it, he put in such a terrific string of affidavits, accusing his opponents of false and unjust proceedings under the commission of lunacy, that the court refused to make the order absolute.

Swingsnap, or Swing, as the young counsellor was called, made a hard fight upon the occasion, and one of the judges declared that it was with reluctance he was obliged to decide against him.

" Well," said Gripe, when the moment was over, " I will seal up whatever money I may have left after paying the costs of the lunacy proceedings, and be prepared to hand it over untouched, if a receiver should be granted, as I have no doubt there will."

" Won't you," said Swingsnap, " pay the costs of the present proceedings against us out of what you have on hands, the amount of which I do not know up to this moment?"

" No," replied Gripe ; " that would be disobeying the order of the court, for which I have such a profound respect. The most I can do is, to take out of it the costs incurred in the lunacy proceedings, and the amount of the funeral expences, which will be considerable ; if I touched it after the order of the court, and the refusal of our application, I would be liable to be attached."

" Where, then," said Swingsnap, half choked with suppressed rage, " shall funds be obtained to carry on the suit ?"

" There will, of course," said Gripe, " be a receiver appointed *ad litem*, and perhaps after we have proceeded for a year or so, an allocation order for costs may be made, but until then I must look to you for funds."

"Why," said Swingsnap, inflating his cheeks and foaming at the mouth, "is this the result of our glorious anticipations of gain ? It would have been better that we never had anything to do with this affair."

"It is the law—the law, my dear young friend, which should be always not only obeyed, but reverenced."

"May I ask you," said Swingsnap, still endeavouring to master his feelings, "if you have counted over the gold? You stated that one of your reasons for not including the amount of it in the deed was, that it might be useful to me in entering on my profession, in case claimants should appear from whom it ought to be kept secret. I don't want it now for my own use, but I think you ought to apply it to sustaining our rights in the present proceedings, and, by the way, you never told me yet what the amount was ; perhaps you would favour me with that information now ?"

"Well done, my lawyerling," said Gripe, with a sarcastic sneer ; "well done, by Jove ; there is a young fellow called to the bar, wanting an old, an experienced, a highly respectable solicitor, to violate the law, and leave himself subject to be thrust into prison under an attachment. No, no ; I shall not appropriate funds sealed up by order of the court to any purpose, until that order or injunction be dissolved ; and then as to favouring you with information about the amount, it is not in my power at present. The whole sum is in my safe as I got it, with the exception of the thousand guineas given to the doctor, which, to say the truth, was fairly earned by him. I may add, that as soon as I shall add up my costs, and get the amount of the funeral expenses furnished to me, I will recompense myself out of the sum in hand. I shall then seal up the remainder, and if I should chance to count it, why I may give you the information you require ; but in any case you will have to provide funds for the suit. At the same time, I shall not take a shilling from you but the sums out of pocket. Indeed, I fear, Mr. Swingsnap, that you are infected with the family complaint, inordinate love of money."

"By ——," said Swingsnap, "this is intolerable ; it cannot be borne much longer ; I'd sooner be dead and —— than be obliged to submit to such injustice, coupled, as it is with the grossest insult."

"Calm your fury," said Gripe, "you know your man—if you don't wish to defend the suit, why let it drop to the ground and let the —— of a publican's daughter get the Norberry property, which, in my opinion, amounts to upwards of sixty thousand pounds, exclusive of the trifle which fell into my hands, and which will barely pay me the expenses for the lunacy proceedings and the funeral. Let the matter drop, and I shall be well satisfied ; I am part paid as far as matters have gone, and so, if you please, Mr. Swingsnap, let us cry quits."

He saw the net that was cast aroned him, and that if he attempted to break through it, it would only multiply the difficulties of his case, and with that quick return fron rage to self-possession for which he was so remarkable, he said in a subdued tone, "I promised to obey all your commands, and submit my judgment to yours, and I don't know why it is that I have not proper command over myself : proceed in your defence in the suit, and any assistance I can give shall be freely granted."

"Ah ! my dear young friend," said Gripe, shaking him warmly by the hand, "my expectations of your high promise as a lawyer shall not be disappointed : I withdraw any thing harsh that I said of you a moment ago, and I now undertake not to ask money from you but as you can conveniently give it, and if you do not succeed in the end, I shall make a present of the amount of my costs, except the money out of pocket."

Swingsnap thanked him, and they were apparently friends again, although a deep-rooted enmity to each other existed in the breasts of both. Gripe took the most active measures for the defence, and after nearly three years litigation, the suit was terminated in the manner already described, and during its progress

Swingsnap advanced various sums of money to defray the expenses out of pocket.

Within a few months after the death of the heir, and complete triumph over Wormwood, Swinsnap thought it time to have a settlement with his solicitor, and all particulars ascertained with regard to the amount of his uncle's property, for he was till then in perfect ignorance upon the subject, except as far as rumour went. In the meantime the best possible understanding existed between himself an Gripe. Entertainments to celebrate their good fortune were respectively given by them, at which large numbers of the leading men of Dublin were present. However, the day of reckoning should come at last, and as long accounts about money matters are always difficult to settle, and very often lead to ill feelings and animosities between old friends, it was easy to foresee that transactions such as occurred between Gripe and his client would be rather difficult to arrange, and the more delay of course the more difficulty. He repeatedly called for the bill of costs which he knew he would have to pay, and which he suspected would be growing plethoric in proportion to the time it might remain unfurnished; but Gripe always postponed the matter under one pretence or another, until his client completely lost his usual patience. Whilst in this state of mind he called one day at his office, and in presence of two or three of his clerks he said, "Mr. Gripe, I cannot brook this delay any longer; I must have the costs furnished, credit given for the sums paid by me whilst the suit was going on, and an accurate account returned of the money and securities which you got into your possession the day my unfortunate uncle was sent to the asylum."

"What money are you talking of?" said Gripe. "I have no recollection of what you allude to, and now, in the absence of documents and vouchers, I cannot at this moment tax my memory with having received any money for any particular purpose."

He felt almost electrified; but with that habitual command which he had over himself, he affected a smile, and said, "I see, Mr. Gripe, you are in a joking humour to-day, and I must only call on you when you are more serious and inclined to speak about business."

"Oh, my dear friend," said Gripe, "you dine with me to-day, and perhaps we may talk of business afterwards; but you know it has been a good business for you, and you ought to be well satisfied to let matters rest as they are for some time."

"Let it be so," said Swingsnap, "but most undoubtedly the bill of costs must be furnished without any further delay, and perhaps you might as well just now direct one of your clerks to run his eye over the account, and see at a hasty tot, without taking in the shillings or pence, how much money I gave you whilst the suit was going on—that is, what credits I am entitled to on foot of your entire claim against me."

"Well, bless my soul," said Gripe, "I thought we were to say nothing about accounts at present; but you have such a *penchant* for making inquiries about money that I foresee you will die rich. But, before you go further, sign this declaration, and put this yellow boy in your pocket." Here he handed him a guinea.

He viewed the coin, turned it two or three times in his hand, and after striking it on the desk beside him, in order to judge of its genuineness by its sound, he relaxed the stern countenance he had assumed, and put it in his pocket.

The clerks who had been in the office when the conversation about credits and bills of costs commenced, were called away about business, and the attorney and client were alone together. "My young friend," said Gripe, "let me now take this opportunity to give you a short lesson that may be useful as well to a barrister as to an attorney. It is this: if ever you are questioned before witness with regard to sums of money received by you, never admit anything. The memory of man is very frail with regard to matters of detail or minute facts; but there can be no mistake where nothing is admitted, in fact where everything is denied. If I happened to say before a man of a weak memory or muddy intellect, that

I got a hundred pounds, he might multiply it by five, and still think he was telling the truth; but where there is a general and uniform denial at all times, there can be no mistake about it, and no man can ever pick an *assumpsit* out of you." Here the worthy attorney looked round the room, and having closed the door, continued: "To be sure, I have got several large sums of money from you, all of which you shall get credit for; the money too which I received on the day that your uncle was sent to the asylum shall be fairly accounted for to the last

shilling. You will not then, my dear friend, find fault with me for not deviating from one of the most useful rules ever observed by any member of the legal profession, and indeed I might add, by all men in their transactions with one another."

Gripe, as he finished the sentence, rubbed his hands briskly together, and, affecting a smile, advanced towards Swingsnap, who turned about and flew out of the room, uttering a most terrific oath, as he banged the door after him, that he would be no longer the victim of such villany and deceit. Gripe, who was astonished at the sudden, although not altogether unexpected change which affairs were likely to take, ran to the street after his client, but he had disappeared. A messenger was then despatched to his house, with a request that he should return, until he might hear one word by way of explanation, but he had not gone home.

The attorney had some friends to dine with him that day, and amongst the rest a Connaught gentleman named Kirwin, who was then one of the most celebrated fire-eaters amongst the pugnacious sons of the West. The occurrence that took place between himself and Swingsnap put him in a fit of abstraction that made him almost forget the names of the visitors; and when Kirwin, who was one of the first who had arrived, entered the reception room, he mistook him for another gentleman who was to form one of the company, and who was as remarkable for his quiet and peaceable conduct as the other was for his fighting propensities.

"Why," said Kirwin, "what is the matter with you? You look as lachrymose as if you were to be shivering on a daisy to-morrow. I did not look half so minister-like the evening before I fought my forty-seventh duel, although that is an unlucky number, and many friends whom I knew went on gloriously till they came to it, and then they were sure to be hit. However, I passed the rubicon, and I can never be vanquished."

"What," said Gripe, in a hurried and excited voice, "put the thought of duelling and shooting into your head at this moment? Did you hear anything that would lead you to think that I by any possibility could be engaged in such an affair?"

"No, by my honour I did not," replied Kirwin; "but I see that there is 'an affair' either in hands or in _petto_;" and then dashing over towards his host and tapping him playfully on the shoulder: "We will have fine fun, I promise you, by —— we will; I'll be your man, and it appears to me most fortunate that I came here to-day."

The remainder of the guests arrived immediately afterwards, dinner passed over, and the gentlemen having sent the decanters through four or five circulating courses, were mellow and merry when a thundering knock came to the door.

"I smell fire in that knock, by ——," said Kirwin; "the applicant for admission is on fighting business, I'd bet a rump and dozen; hurrah for fun!"

Gripe looked pale, and observed to Kirwin that his merriment was of a very heartless character.

"What is it all about?" said one and the other of the guests. "Who is to breakfast on bullets?" said an old attorney named Irwin, as he placed a glass of "bee's wing" between him and the light; "it is not my friend Gripe, I am sure, for although he is considered one of the best sharpshooters in his profession, I know he prefers parchment to powder; and as to you, Kirwin, no man would have anything to do with you except he wished to commit suicide in a respectable way. With regard to the rest of the company, I can answer for them that they are not fighting men, and no one would send any of them a message, so that you must be mistaken."

"Many a message sent on such a speculation," said Kirwin.

"Then you are not the man for whom such an invitation could be intended," replied Irwin.

Here the servant came into the room almost breathless.

"What is the matter, Robert?" said Gripe.

"Oh! sir, there is a gentleman in the small back-palour, who told me he would not leave the house until he had seen you. I said first you were not at home, and he told me you were. I then said that you never saw any one after dinner, and he replied that he would not go without seeing you. I am sure, sir he means nothing good; he has the very —— in his countenance, and I'd advise you, sir, not to see him. I'll call the groom to help me to put him out."

"Who is right?" said Kirwin, exultingly. "Did not I tell you there was fire in the knock? But take care let no insult be offered to the gentleman. I would feel myself disgraced for ever if any man coming about 'an affair of honour to the house of a friend where I happened to be, should be treated improperly. We must see what he is about; and I promise you he will have to pull down his colours, or fighting Jack Kirwin is not a living man."

Gripe, who was at first inclined to act upon the suggestion of the servant, felt that if he did so he would only raise up another opponent, perhaps still more dangerous, so he thought it better to secure the friendship and assistance of Kirwin in the matter, in the hope that he would become the principal himself. "Kirwin," said he, "I must leave this matter in your hands. I am certain that the gentleman who now wishes to see me is the bearer of a hostile message from a client of mine, who wishes to shoot me to get rid of a bill of costs."

"Who is he?" said Kirwin.

"That graceless villain, young Swingsnap the lawyer," replied Gripe.

"A good shot, by Jupiter," replied Kirwin, "and a fellow who has been often heard to declare that he would fight his way to promotion; but he has not experience, so we need not be afraid."

"Oh! I won't fight him," said Gripe, "for the reasons I tell you; he owes me a large bill of costs, and if he took me down by a chance shot he fancies the debt would be paid, and if I should shoot him I will lose my money."

"That apology won't avail you," said Kirwin, "unless the dispute out of which the message arose was concerning the debt due by your challenger."

"That is exactly what occurred. He called on me relative to those costs, and thought to get admissions from me before my clerks that he paid me large sums of money in liquidation of them, whereas I never got a shilling from him; it was a perpetual outlay on my part, and when I insisted upon getting money even on account, it appears that the reply is an invitation to fight him."

"You are safe then," replied Kirwin, "if that be the exact state of the case. You need not fight him till your demand is satisfied."

"I know that such is the etiquette," said Gripe," "and I would thank you if you would see this fire-eating gentleman on my part, and give him his answer."

"You must see him yourself first, and then refer him to me as your friend."

"Very well," replied Gripe, "but this I am determined on—there shall be no duel."

"Well, then," rejoined Kirwin, "don't refer him to me, for I am determined that there shall, if there ought; but as the matter stands at present it is not likely that there will."

Gripe retired from the company, and repaired to meet his new visitor, but he was almost electrified with surprise when he opened the door of the apartment, and beheld his old antagonist and relentless enemy, Wormwood. He supposed at first that he had come upon some matter connected with the former litigation, but his mistake was soon corrected by the following salutation:

"You did not expect to meet me in your own house, Mr. Gripe, and above all you did not expect to have met me upon business unconnected with our profession."

"What, then, may your business be?" said Gripe, interrupting him; "but let me tell you that, whatever it is, you had great effrontery to come into my house. Come, sir, take yourself away in an instant."

"No, sir, I shall not take myself away until I discharge the duty I owe to my friend who sent me here. I have come, sir, on the part of Mr. Swingsnap, whom you first defrauded, and then insulted—at least he states so to me, and you know does not require much proof to convince me of the fact; but these are all lateral matters. My friend has been insulted, and I am come to arrange a meeting. Put me at once in communication with your friend; my instructions are peremptory—no apology will be taken."

"There is none going to be offered," said Gripe; "but no message shall be received at your hands. Let any gentleman come here, and I shall refer him to a friend in an instant; he is here in the house; but I may as well tell you that Swingsnap shall have no shot at me until he discharges the heavy debt that he owes me. Ruffians are not to get rid of their liabilities by shooting their creditors. Come sir, leave my house instantly."

"Do you refuse to receive a message at my hands?" said Wormwood. "Mark me, if you do, I shall make it personal with myself, and you must fight me."

"I would as soon meet a felon from Newgate," replied Gripe, "but let your new friend send any man of character here, and the matter will be speedily arranged. Come leave my house, sir, instantly."

Wormwood was maddened to desperation; words ran high; abusive epithets were applied by one, and back with interest by the other, until the attention of Kirwin and the party in the dining-room was attracted, and they all ran out to the hall, where the belligerent parties had by this time arrived, to see what was the matter.

When Wormwood saw this reinforcement, inflated as they were with wine, he began to think it would have been much better for him to have taken the advice even of an enemy, and to have left the house when directed to do so; but Kirwin quieted his fears by proposing at once to become an arbitrator of the preliminary matter in dispute, namely, whether his friend Gripe could refuse receiving a message through Wormwood any more than any other person; and, lawyer-like, he insisted that a deed of submission should be executed, by both parties promising, unconditionally, to abide by his decision.

Gripe believed that the fame of Kirwin as a fire-eater would overawe Wormwood. and not wishing to raise up a new enemy where he might have a friend who, for the splitting of a hair, would stand a shot in his place, pledged his honour to be guided entirely by his advice.

"Let me hear," said Kirwin, "why you refuse to receive a message by this gentleman, or rather to put him in communication with your friend, who is to judge, whether you are to fight or not,"

"I have had," replied Gripe, "to do with this person professionally, and his conduct was so ungentlemanly, and, I will add, fraudulent, that I could not think of admitting him to the position of a gentleman; and besides that, he was kicked out of a public court in Wexford, and he did not resent it."

"If the latter fact be true," said Kirwin, "he is totally disqualified from acting either as principal or second, as no gentleman could hold intercourse with him, but as to frauds committed by one attorney upon another in their professional career, they cannot be recognised, unless the unoffending party be disgraced by a trial and conviction, or degraded by the judges of the courts where he practises. Has either of these things been done?"

"Neither, I admit," said Gripe; "but that he deserved to be degraded is capable of proof."

"Have the acts you complain of been confined to his practise as an attorney?"

"They have."

"The judges of the courts where he practises did not take cognizance of them?"

"No."

"Nor can I; so that point is disposed of. But now, as to having been kicked and not resenting it, he has earned another kicking by coming here, and I am the very man to pay what is due in that respect."

"That is more than can be said of you in other respects," said old Irwin, who had, with the rest of the company, come to witness what was going on. "It wou[ld] be a rare thing to see you pay your bill when due."

"Never mind that, my old cock," said Kirwin. "You are a Connaught-man yourself, and those who live in glass houses ought not to be the first to throw stones."

"True for you," said Irwin; "but if we don't pay in money we pay in malt. I recollect that a pedlar to whom my father once owed half-a-crown came looking for it, and he kept him six months at his house, living in prime style, sooner than pay him in money. The fellow went dealing through the country by day, and came every night to Castle Irwin to eat, and drink, and sleep, all upon the strength of the half-crown. At length, when my poor father died, the rascally pedlar actually sued me, as heir, for the debt which was a thousand times discharged, and I had to pay it with costs, amounting to ten times more than the original demand."

"Come, come," said Kirwin, "none of your old stories just now; I will listen to them with great pleasure over a glass of claret, as soon as this little affair is settled, which I trust will be speedily, as obstacle number one is already got over." Then turning to Wormwood, "Have you, sir, been kicked out of a public court in Wexford by a gentleman, without calling him out? Be explicit, sir, tell the truth; if you admit you were, I shall merely apply my boot in a gentle way to the ignoble portion of your person, and never think of you again; but if you falsely deny it, I shall not only horsewhip you like a dog in the first public place I meet you, but you shall be posted as a liar and a coward throughout England, Ireland, Scotland, and France."

"I will suffer all that ignominy without a complaint," replied Wormwood, "if there be any truth in the assertion."

"Upon what authority," said Kirwin to Gripe, "have you made this statement?"

"I have it from the coroner of Wexford, who told me that Wormwood was so grossly offensive and ruffianly in his court that he had to order him to be kicked out, or did it himself; I am not positive which."

"A dignified judge that," replied Kirwin; "but you ought to know, Mr. Gripe, that even if he did so, the party whom he treated with such indignity could no more call him out for it than he could call out one of the judges off the bench —many of whom are so testy and unmannerly, that were it not for the legal shield which shelters them, I would myself have called out every man-jack of them long since. The coroner, whilst discharging the duties of his office—no matter how he performs them—is *de jure* a judge, and cannot be called out, no matter what fantastic tricks he plays before high Heaven whilst so employed; that is a settled point in the code of honour, and sending a message to a man whom that code does not recognise as amenable to its laws would be considered as an act of cowardice; so there is obstacle the second got rid of."

"Well, then," said Gripe, "you know the third and insuperable one. A heavy debt is not to be got rid of by shooting the creditor. My demand against Swingsnap must be satisfied before you receive any hostile message from him on my account."

"Is the exact amount of your demand ascertained?" inquired Kirwin.

"I know something of the transactions between the parties," answered Wormwood; "and I will forfeit all I am possessed of on earth, if, on a settlement of accounts, there would not be found a heavy balance on the other side."

"Mere assertions of either party cannot decide that point," observed Kirwin; "but that a demand was made by my friend is beyond all doubt, and that a dispute arose in consequence, which led to this message; and until the matter is settled in some way, he need not fight. At the same time, I wish to Heaven I was in his position. When any one owes me money, I generally get it by a proposal to fight or pay. I believe you all recollect the affair of Captain Brummage and myself."

"I have heard something of it," said Irwin; "but mention the facts to us now, for I dare say they are applicable to this case; and if they could serve as a precedent for putting yourself in the position of our friend Gripe, I venture to say he will have no objection to hear them."

"Well, then," continued Kirwin, "I won two hundred guineas from the captain one night at Daly's club-house, and he refused to pay it the next day when I sent for the amount, on the ground that he was drunk when he lost it. I got out of bed when this message was brought me, and having dressed, and put my pistols in order, I waited till I knew the officers would be at mess. I then went to the barrack, and proceeded directly to the mess-room. There was a sentinel at the door, who refused to let me in; so I quietly knocked him down, and passed on. I went up to the mess-table with a pistol in each hand, and demanded my money or an instant meeting with Brummage. The colonel asked what was the matter, and I told him that one of his officers refused to pay a debt, under the disgraceful apology that he was drunk when it was contracted. It is unnessary to give a detail of all that was said; but the sequel of the story was, that I left the room with my money in my pocket."

"I believe," said Gripe, "that Swingsnap would suffer to be shot, and go to a hot place after, sooner than pay a just debt."

"Then," replied Kirwin, "what may be the amount of your demand against him ?"

"There is a long unsettled account between us, and I could not tell at this moment."

"Well, then, after all due credits given, how much, at a rough guess, would you be entitled to ?"

"I really think that two thousand pounds would hardly pay me, after giving credit for any trifle that may have come into my hands."

"The matter can be easily arranged," said Kirwin. "You admit that there is an unsettled account, and that there may be about two thousand pounds due to you on foot of it. I propose, then, that that sum be lodged by your challenger in the hands of a mutual friend, to abide the settlement; that, if it be found due to you, it shall be handed over to you or your heirs; if not, that it be returned to the party depositing it. This arrangement will put you on an equal footing; and if it be agreed to by the gentleman who has brought me the message, I at once arrange a meeting for five to-morrow morning."

Gripe stared about him with a kind of half frantic amazement, and was unable to utter a sentence in reply; but Wormwood, who knew very well how the facts of the case were, agreed at once to the proposal. He said, he happened to have so much money in his house, and he would, within an hour, deposit it in the hands of any solvent and respectable gentleman who might be agreed upon.

"You have acted like a man of honour," said Kirwin. "There is a satisfaction in doing business with you. Go lodge the money and make your arrangements. I shall make mine, and be punctual to the moment at five in the morning, Hurrah, we will have some fun. Come, Gripe, my boy, cheer up; if you only follow my advice you will pink your man. Come, for another bottle of whiskey, and then I'l preach a sermon—hush, hurrah !"

I am a young fellow
Who loves to be mellow,
To drink and be merry is all my delight ;
I often get frisky,
By tippling good whiskey,
With jovial companions, from morning to night.
I never took pleasure
In hoarding up treasure ;
The sight of a miser I cannot endure,
Who always is griping,
And sharping and biting,
And laying out schemes to plunder the poor
Ri fal-da-riddle lah, &c.

Of the beggerly miser
I am a despiser;
The fruit of his labour he never enjoys;
His heirs for his money,
Impatient of honey,
Are waiting and hate him, while with it he toys.
His frame is complaining,
For want of sustaining;
His limbs are decrepit from hunger and cold;
Instead of good liquor
To make his pulse quicker.
He's gloating and doting on that idol called gold.
Ri fal," &c.

" Well," said Kirwin to. Gripe, "I believe I have m anaged that matter to your satisfaction. Your bill of costs will be secured before we go to the ground. I'm the boy for bringing forgetful gentlemen to their recollection. Come, push around the whiskey before we proceed to make arrangements for the morning."

"You totally mistake the character of my opponent," said Gripe. "He will never pay a shilling. He has inherited some of the qualities of his old uncle along with his wealth. Money is his God, and he would willingly go to a hot place that shall be nameless, sooner than pay anything he could by possibility avoid."

"Then," replied Kirwin, "if you be in doubt of getting the amount of your demand in any case, you should feel the less regret at shooting him."

"I think you were too hasty in your arrangements," rejoined Gripe ; "but I know the money won't be lodged this evening or at any other time, and that there will be, therefore, no duel."

"Don't, my dear friend, anticipate such a dissapointment," said Kirwin. "But this I tell you, that there must be a duel in any case. That snubnosed attorney— who, I must say, has, up to our parting, acted in the most gentlemanly way—told me that he had the money in his own house ready to deposit, that he would do so this evening, and if he does not bring me the receipt of Mr. Gaskin, into whose hands it has been agreed to put it, I shall call himself out in the morning for having dared to tell me a lie."

Whilst Gripe was indulging in the conjecture that the money would not be lodged, and Kirwin resolving in his own mind that in any event there should be a shot, a thundering knock came to the door.

"The money is lodged," said Kirwin ; "that is the knock of the gentleman who was here awhile ago."

Gripe trembled and turned pale, but said nothing.

"The gentleman who was here this evening," said the servant, as he opened hte door, "wishes to see Mr. Kirwin."

"Quite at his service," said Kirwin," starting from his chair. The interview between him and Wormwood was short. The money had been lodged, and a copy of the receipt put into his hands, with which he returned exulting to his friends in the dining-room. "All has been satisfactorily arranged," said he, as he entered. "Send at once for my pistols till we have some practice, and get them in order for the morning. I'll make my friend Gripe snuff a candle to-night before I part him." The pistols were accordingly sent for, and Kirwin having placed a candle with a "heavy snuff" opposite an open window, so as to afford an exit for the bullet, he stood at the other side of the room, and at the first shot actually topped it clean.

"My hand is always steady," said he, "after a good bottle of wine, and I wish it was the practice to fight duels in the evening ; there is something too sober and steady about those morning affairs ; but my plan is always to make an evening of the morning on which I either fight or act as second. I keep it up till within a few minutes of going to the ground. I propose then that we have a supper, and while it is in preparation we will see what my friend can do. Place the other candle on the table, and take this pistol and have a whack at it."

Gripe saw that a duel was inevitable, and having arranged the second candle in the place of the first, he took the pistol into his trembling hand.

"Come," said Kirwin, uttering a horrible oath, "if you betray such fears when we go to the ground in the morning, I will look upon it as an insult, take the place of your antagonist, and riddle you in a thrice. I will by —— ; so mark that. Just hear me for a moment, and follow the advice I shall give. In the first place, believe most firmly in your own mind that you'l pink your man: let that be your firm impression. In the next place, cock your own trigger—it steadies the hand; raise your arm gently, still keeping the elbow resting on your body; keep your eye on your mark ; level, so as to strike about the knee ; be quick in firing when the signal is made, and you will surely hit him about the groin. There are other instructions for hitting higher, but those I have given are the safest for a new beginner. I once met a fellow whom I did not like to hit, and I put a ball through his hat about half an inch above his head. I was originally in the wrong, and after the first shot, offered to make an apology, but the fellow would not take it, and I had no resource left but to hit him ; he died on the spot, and I had to fly to France for a year till the thing was forgotten."

Gripe summoned all the fortitude he could command to his aid, and having followed the directions given by his friend, he let fly at the candle, and, struck the candlestick.

A shout of triumph from Kirwin made the house ring, and supper having been soon after served up, the party began to spend the evening.

"Blessings on the man," said Kirwin, "who invented poteen! it brings one's heart into the mouth ; it's better than an outside coat ; it makes one speak out, and care not a fig for the pope, the priest, or the devil."

Gripe perceiving there was no retreating from the position he was placed in, was obliged to make up his mind to fight, and when Wormwood withdrew, he retired with his friends to the dining-room.

Kirwin, who felt quite comfortable, said he would not return home until after the affair came off, and two others of the company, one an heir just come of age, for whom Gripe had been solicitor during his minority, came to a similar resolution. The other gentlemen said they had no curiosity to see any man shot, and they took their leave when supper was over, wishing their host a safe deliverance.

The four gentleman who remained kept the glass slowly circulating till the clock struck four.

"Those sounds won't be heard again," said Kirwin, "till this affair shall be ended. I am always a few seconds before the appointed hour. Five by my watch is the time appointed, and I have it some minutes in advance. That clock won't strike again till all is over."

Gripe made no reply, and a coach which had been ordered immediately after Wormwood's visit the previous evening, drove to the door, and the four gentlemen entered it.

It was a delightful summer's morning, and as they passed through college-green by the Post-office, they saw it was but four o'clock by the town.

"We are too soon on the road," said Gripe; "my clock is a great deal too fast,"

"I put it forward last night," replied Kirwin, "that I might have you out in good time. It is one 'of my rules to be first on the field, that I may have an opportunity of examining the ground, and see what its advantages are."

The post-office clock chimed the hour, and all the clocks of the city were heard in quick succession; the atmosphere was clear, the morning calm, and there being no sound in the streets, the sounds were heard with perfect distinctness, and broke upon the ear of Gripe as if his funeral knell had been ringing. There is something peculiarly awful in the tolling of a bell or the striking of a clock just before a man places himself at a gentlemanly distance to be fired at, merely to uphold some imaginary point of honour ; the one is generally a summons to prayer, and the other tells us that we are hastening to the boundary between time and eternity, thus reminding a man of the summons before the judgment seat, and of the speedy termination which he is likely to put to his earthly career.

The party proceeded by the old toll-house, and through Donnybrook, to a field a little beyond it on the Stillorgan road. The sun had risen in the golden splendour of a July morning; the birds were singing the praises of their Creator in varied notes; the Wicklow men were coming into market with their butter and

provisions of all kinds, whistling merrily, whilst seated behind their panniers, or driving their low-wheeled cars. Every thing bore the aspect of happiness and rejoicing; it was the *formosissimus annus* of the poet, when every field and tree was in bloom, and every object proclaimed the benevolence, as well as the omnipotence of the Deity. Yet man will impiously dare to defile the earth with the blood of his fellow-man, and destroy as far as his limited powers enable him, that harmony and peace which should exist in unison with the glories of creation. This is called honour, and those who thus wilfully transgress the ordinances of

No. 11.

God and the laws of their country, have hitherto been looked upon as the *elite* of society; but the spirit of religion and the love of morality are, thank Heaven, now too prevalent in almost every country, to permit such a feeling to continue, and the duellist is now looked upon almost with universal accord as the most degraded, immoral, and contemptible of the human race.

Kirwin had his man first on the ground, and with the eye of an old practitioner viewed the field where the parties were so soon to meet in deadly combat. He was but a few moments making his observations, when a carriage drove up containing Swingsnap, Wormwood, and a surgeon.

"I always like," said Kirwin, " to see gentlemen bring their bone-setters with 'em; it is a proof that they don't expect to go home in a whole skin, and it proves also that they are determined to die game." Then stepping up to Wormwood he shook him warmly by the hand, observing at the same time that he felt much indebted to him for the business-like manner in which he had conducted the whole case.

"You see we are in earnest." said Wormwood; "my friend is determined not to leave the field till one or other falls. He says he wishes to rid the world of a villain like Gripe."

"What do you mean?" said Kirwin. "That is an insult intended for me. Do you think, sir, that I, who was the second of eleven lords, nine marquises, and twenty-seven captains, and who fought and shot so many men of rank myself, would come out as the friend of a villain? Take your position, sir, at once, till you and I settle our affair before the other goes on."

The countenance of poor Gripe, who stood at a distance with his mouth closely shut to keep his teeth from chattering, brightened up, and he kindly proposed to act as the second of Kirwin, for he believed that, if Wormwood were shot, there would be an end of his danger.

"Oh, my dear sir," said the terrified attorney, "I meant no disrespect to you; I solemnly protest I did not, and I tender you the most ample apology that it is in my power to give."

"It must be in writing," replied Kirwin; "I must have the *litera scripta*; I will frame it, and hang it up over my chimney piece, where I have many others."

Here some difficulty occurred with regard to procuring writing materials; but no entreaty could prevail upon Kirwin to leave the ground until an apology according to his own dictatation was written and given to him by Wormwood.

The distance was then measured, and the original belligerents placed in their respective positions. There was a bold determination and apparent recklessness of consequences about Swingsnap, that formed a strong contrast to the downcast appearance and ashy paleness of Gripe, whose legs tottered under him as he was led to his place by his second.

"Remember," said Kirwin, "the instructions I gave you last night, and the candlestick."

But his words fell listlessly upon the ear of Gripe, who was in such terror and bewilderment that he was almost unconscious of everything that passed. Swingsnap, with his usual coolness and determination, saw the condition of his adversary, and gained confidence in proportion to the terror which he manifested.

The fatal signal was given—Swingsnap fired first—his adversary raised his pistol, and, at the moment he discharged it, his hand quivered, he reeled backwards, and fell; he was hit in the hip. Wormwood saw that his work was accomplished to his satisfaction, and lest he might get involved in further disputes with Kirwin, which would end in placing him in a similar position to his old enemy, he ran with his principal to the carriage that was waiting, and drove off, leaving Kirwin, the surgeon, and the other gentlemen who had come out to witness the proceedings, to attend the unfortunate Gripe.

"Bad business," said Kirwin; "I was never more deceived in my life; but there are some men who will not profit by instructions, and if they do not, the fault is theirs and not their instructors; had he followed my advice, he would, beyond all doubt, have winged his man. To be sure, his opponent might be equally well instructed, and when that is the case both fall, and then there's a glorious termination of the duel; but is he badly wounded?"

"I fear so," replied the surgeon; "I find that the ball has entered under the hip, and is lodged in the lower regions of the abdomen. There is litle hope of his recovery."

"Is that villain Kirwin there?" said Gripe, faintly; "I will leave my deat on him, and in my dying moments declare that he brought me out here to be shot."

Kirwin uttered an exclamation of surprise at what he called the ingratitude of his friend, accompanied with a litany of the most terrible oaths, and feeling that the consequences might be very serious, as the authorities of the day were most anxious for an opportunity to rid society of him, he gained the carriage in which he and his friends came out, and having gone home and hastily packed up his clothes, he drove to Ringsend, and got on board the Holyhead packet, on his way to France, where he was mortally wounded in a gambling-house the following year by a Frenchman, whom he refused to fight except with his favourite weapons, pistols. The Frenchman declined the pistol combat, and, in his fury, drove the sword through him.

Gripe was conveyed home in a state that gave little hope of his recovery. The duel made a great noise in Dublin; report had it that the notorious fire-eater Kirwin, brought him out to be shot; the circumstances of the case were told in a thousand different ways, and no event of the kind ever caused more gossip among the quidnuncs of Dublin. The authorities, however, took no step towards the prosecution of Swingsnap or his second, and the recollection of the matter soon died away.

It was feared that the wound of Gripe was mortal; he daily became worse; and an ineffectual attempt to extract the ball left not a glimpse of hope of his recovery. On the ninth day mortification set in, and in one of these intervals of repose which immediately precede death, he called his apprentice into the room, and desired him to write down as he would dictate. He wished that society might profit by his history, but above all, that he might leave some evidence after him that would aid in exposing the infamy of Swingsnap, and bringing him to justice.

CHAPTER VIII.

CONFESSION AND END OF GRIPE.—DEATH OF BLIND TIM.

"I was," said Gripe, "the son of a village apothecary, was originally intended for that profession, and was accordingly sent to the school of one of those fugitive priests who then lurked in the country, endeavouring to support themselves by clandestinely instructing those who wished to acquire classical learning at a nominal expense, or in many cases for nothing, as those who were fraudulent enough to take advantage of the circumstances in which those persecuted men were placed, need not pay them anything; for if it were known to the public authorities that they dared to keep a school or instruct youth, they would be transported, and I am sorry to say that my father was one of those who availed themselves of this advantage; for although I was about three years off and on at school with this priest, he was never paid a penny. The poor man lived in the house of a protestant in humble circumstances, who interested himself in getting pupils for him, and under his protection he was enabled to escape the fangs of the 'priest hunters.' I remember him well—he was a venerable-looking old man, with long white hair, and in the mud-walled hut where he had his school, he appeared as happy with a few ragged urchins about him, as if he were in the enjoyment of wealth and every earthly comfort. Notwithstanding his truly benevolent character, I took a dislike to him, because he frequently expressed his fears that some evil end would come of me, I was so mischievous and incorrigible. The poor man was unwilling to correct any of his pupils, lest their parents should be offended or attention drawn in any way to his little school; in a word, he felt that he was living on sufferance, and indebted to his neighbours, many of them protestants, for his existence, and this, added to his kindness of disposition, prevented him from exercising the authority or enforcing the obedience necessary for conducting a school with profit to the pupils. I was one of those who took advantage of the unfortunate man's circumstances, and was always doing something to torment him. One day I mounted the hut in which the school was kept, and through a hole in the roof that answered the double purpose of chimney and window, I let fall a stone on his bare head that stunned him so much that he fell bleeding on the floor. He was carried to the house of his benefactor, and there confined to his bed till he died of a fracture in his skull, caused by that infamous act. The poor man was privately buried near the ruins of an old abbey, a short distance from where he kept his school. It may be worthy of remark, that Edgeworth, which was the name of his protestant benefactor, was in a short time after informed against for harbouring a popish priest, and had to fly the country to escape a government prosecution. With regard to myself, it is right to say that I was, after the commission of the diabolical deed just stated, held in utter execration by every one. My old school-fellows, both protestant and catholic, shunned me as they would a plague; yet no one would speak of the matter publicly, lest attention might be directed towards Edgeworth, who, notwithstanding, was unable to escape the informers of the day.

"I felt that I was an outcast to society, that every man was my enemy; and I in return was determined that, whilst I kept a fair face to all, I should never miss an opportunity of doing all the injury in my power to my fellow-man: in a word, I was at war with the world, and the world was at war with me. My father, who, in common with all country apothecaries, was dignified with the title of doctor, took me as an apprentice, to instruct me in making boluses and compounding his own prescriptions.

"He was a tolerable chemist, and having a small laboratory on his premises, I took great delight in making those common experiments which are so amusing and mysterious to the uninitiated, and in attempting new ones that I fancied might lead to some discovery that would make my fortune. My father had Latin translations of the writings of some of the German magi and the philosophers who spent so much of their time in seeking for the philosopher's stone, or *vitae elixir*, which, thanks to the poor priest whose death I caused, I was able to read with tolerable facility. Some two or three years thus passed away at my favourite pursuits.

"I was seldom seen in the shop, and when my father's absence made it indispensible that I should be there, I saw that the people regarded me with aversion, which I paid back with compound interest whenever an opportunity suited; but a circumstance occurred which broke up our establishment, and sent me to act my part in scenes of a different character.

"My father was absent one day, when the servant of a neighbouring farmer came for him in great haste to attend his son, a young lad of fifteen or sixteen, who had a violent bleeding from the nose. Not finding him at home, the messenger insisted that I should go and administer to him all the relief in my power. I at first refused peremptorily; for this boy, who was one of my former school-fellows, had, from the time of the priest affair, treated me with the greatest contempt and scorn. On one occasion, when there were some strolling showmen in the village, I went to the exhibition, and this lad, with the boys of a school at which he then was, came in, but when he saw me on a seat near them, he induced them all to leave the place and remain outside as long as I remained inside.

"I vowed vengeance in my own mind, although I never seemed to notice the circumstance. My mother—who I may here say was a religious but weak woman, to whom I was the cause of perpetual grief—induced me to go with the messenger, if I did no more than bring back word to my father, who was expected home in a few hours, what the condition of the boy was. I mounted the horse that the messenger brought, and when I arrived at my destination, I met the father of the boy at the door, who seemed utterly surprised at seeing me.

"'What brought you here?' said he, 'you graceless ruffian. I thought you had quit the country long ago. Begone! I would as soon let Belzebub near my child.'

"I did not make a reply; and when I returned home I said nothing of the reception I had got, but merely observed to my mother, that I was deemed too young and inexperienced to prescribe on such an occasion. My father arrived in a few minutes after me, and without waiting for any refreshment he hurried off to see the patient. He returned quickly, and wrote a prescription for the lad, which I was to compound. I set about the task assigned me, and contrived to mix with the materials a deadly poison, then but recently discovered, the effects of which it would be very difficult to detect upon an analysis of the stomach.

"I need hardly say what the result was; but a proceeding followed, which ended in the ruin of my father and my banishment from the country. He was prosecuted for having administered poison to the child, and was acquitted; but his establishment was broken up, and the poor man died in the course of a year afterwards, a victim to my infamy and crime. The infamous notoriety I had acquired did not, however, extend beyond the town where we lived, and its immediate vicinity, and I resolved to proceed to Dublin to seek my fortune; and in case I did not succeed there, I determined to cross the Atlantic to America, which had at that time but recently established its independence.

"My mother was in the receipt of the rent of a couple of small houses in the town, which removed her above absolute want, and she allowed me to dispose of the shop fixtures and bottles in the best way I could, and take the proceeds with me. The produce of the sale amounted to twenty pounds some odd shillings, and with this sum in my pocket, and a small valise under my arm, I left home before daylight on an autumn morning, and walked out of the town before the fly-van, as it was called, although it travelled only at the rate of about three miles an hour, and in which I had previously engaged a seat under another name.

"When I got into the vehicle, I found in it two shopkeepers of the town, who were proceeding to Dublin to purchase goods, and such was their horror at seeing me, that they insisted upon my being put out of it; the matter was, however, accommodated by my taking my seat outside with the driver. I said nothing in reply to the aspersions they had then cast upon me, but took out my memorandum book, and coolly wrote down their names, with a *nota bene* at the bottom, 'I will one day or other be revenged.'

"I arrived in Dublin on the evening of the second day after my departure from home, and put up at a very expensive hotel in James's-street, which was chiefly frequented by country merchants, who came to Dublin to purchase goods from the manufacturers of the Liberty. I fell in that night with some of those persons, and assumed an air of simplicity and candour which I was always well able to assume; at the same time I took the opportunity of displaying my learning and general knowledge of men and things.

"Many of the company were astonished at my acquirements, and began to express a desire to know who I was, where I was going, or for what business I was intended. I told them that my father, who was of high family, and had given me a most expensive education, had recently died in embarrassed circumstances; that I could not bear to be a burthen to my mother, who had a little jointure to support her; and that, trusting to Providence, I had set out to seek my fortune.

" ' You are deserving of support and encouragement,' said a warm, comfortable. looking old fellow, who had come up from Limerick, and who was finishing a large bowl of whiskey punch, which had evidently made him mellow, ' and you must evidently get both.   There is Tarrant the cloth manufacturer, whom I leave some thousands of pounds with in the course of the year, and I think it would be a great acquisition to his trade to have such a young lad as you, who would know how to speak to the people and keep accounts properly.   He has two stupid fellows, who don't know the rule of three, not to talk of book-keeping, and who cannot write a scrawl that a countryman can read.   They are always making mistakes in our accounts, but I err much or you are just the lad that would do everything right.   You have the larnin', what every man ought to have ; and if you have no objection, I will introduce you to Tarrant to-morrow.'

" To be brief with this part of my recital, it may be sufficient to say, that I got an engagement with this manufacturer as corresponding clerk and overseer of a certain department of his trade.   I found that the concern was most prosperous and the receipts of money were enormous, and I was resolved to conduct myself, with the greatest propriety until I could get into the office of cashier to the establishment.   I saw that my employer, although immensely rich, was of the most niggardly and parsimonious habits, and I pursued a course which I was certain would at once win his confidence.   If I saw a second-hand pen being swept out of the office by the porter, I would take it up, observing, that it would bear another mending, and that there was no use in waste.   On Sundays there was always wine on the table, with which the rest of the clerks made pretty free, but I declined to taste it, on the ground that it was not fit for a young lad who was cast upon the world to seek his fortune to accustom himself to such expensive things.

" My master was highly delighted at this conduct, and frequently observed to his wife that he always knew his customer, old Roach of Limerick, who had recommended me to him, to be a man of discernment.   He called me one day into his private office, and submitted to me the cashier's account, in which I detected two errors, and although they were afterwards cleared up, he seemed not to be satisfied, and frequently told me that he only waited for an opportunity to raise me to the office which I secretly coveted.

" The cashier was a man of discernment, and saw at once into my character, but I was such a favourite with my master he did not venture to state his opinion of me, more particularly as he was aware that it was I who discovered the errors in his accounts, and that if he threw out any insinuations against me they would be attributed to malicious motives.   He seemed every day to feel more and more uneasy with his situation, or I may rather say with being in such close proximity to me, and upon his marriage, which took place in about a year after I had entered on the duties of my office, an excuse for quitting the service of our employer being afforded him he took advantage of it.

" He was no sooner gone than I was raised to his situation, and for the first three or four months I filled it, nothing could exceed my caution, and, I might add, my honesty, I found, however, that a golden prospect was opened to me.   The free trade of Ireland, which had been some years established, caused a daily increase of business both for home consumption and export to England and America.   Money poured in so abundantly, and orders were so numerous, that our exertions could hardly keep pace with our trade.   I began to filch, and took as occasion might offer, from fifty to two hundred pounds a week out of the receipts of the house.

" During this period there was an attorney named Rap, who used to do business for us, and frequently dined with my master, took great notice of me.   He said to me one day that my time and talents were thrown away pinned to a desk in a counting-house, and that if I wished to raise myself in the world I should become a member of his profession.   He added, he thought I was born an attorney, and that if I wished to be authorised to practice a profession for which I was so well suited he would take me without a fee.   He also added, that he had several complicated cases in his office, in the conducting of which my services would be most valuable, and requested that I would consider the offer he had made me.

"I told him that I was so attached to the interests of my master that I did not wish to leave him, and that consideration alone could induce me to hesitate in accepting the kind offer he had made me, although at the same time, I was determined to avail myself of it as soon as I had carried my depredations as far as they could safely go.

"I went on for upwards of two years thus plundering my master, until at length he began to express surprise that the profits were so small where there was such immense business done, and began, when it was rather too late, to express his doubts of my integrity. I saw that the game was nearly up with me, and one day I made a haul of bills and bank notes amounting to something above two hundred pounds. I had taken them out of a desk where there was upwards of two thousand pounds besides, but when I returned after having lodged them in a place of security where the rest of the plunder was, I found that the desk had been opened and the money counted. I ran back and took them again into my possession, and having returned a second time, I threw them under the desk out of which I had originally taken them. I had scarcely this part of my business done when my master came into my office, with rage depicted in his countenance.

"'Gripe,' said he, ' my confidence has been misplaced ; to be at once explicit with you, I tell you that you have been robbing me. I got a second key for your desk; I counted the money and bills last night; I counted them to-day after you went out ; and there was a deficiency of two hundred and twenty pounds.'

"I expressed the most indignant surprise at the accusation, asked him how much he found in it, and desired him to count the money over again. He did count it, and found that it was still deficient to the amount he stated.

"'Why,' said I, 'I had that money out to-day myself, and thought the sum you mention was in it, but I recollect that strong breeze of wind was up the passage that might have blown some o ne notes and bills about the place—did you search? I forgot to search myself at the time, I was so overpowered by the pressure of the business of this establishment, but here, alas! is my reward.'

"A search was made under the desk, and the money of course found. My master semed astounded and confused, but did not express a continuance of his former confidence or withdraw the charge he had made against me."

"I saw that my plundering must cease, and I told him that I should forthwith quit his service, and that he was a specimen of the most base ingratitude. I put on my hat, walked out, and went direct to Rap the attorney, told him the charge that had been made against me, and expressed a wish that he would draw up the form of an affidavit to which I might swear, in order to clear myself. He desired me to take no oath, that no one would believe it, for there was not a thief in existence who would not swear to clear himself; 'but,' added he, ' an indefinite and unproved charge of that kind—in fact the finding of the money disproved anything that was definite in it—will be no bar to my taking you as an apprentice, and the sooner arrangements to that effect are made the better.'

" The indentures were prepared on the following day, I forthwith set to work in the office of Rap, and in an incredibly short time I became one of the most useful and expert men of business he ever had."

It would be perhaps foreign to the purposes for which this confession is intended, to enter into a detail of all the knavery, deceit, and villany that was practised in the office of Rap, or to name the victims who found themselves beggared and ruined at the winding up of their suits, instead of obtaining the rights to which they were entitled. Suffice it to say, that I saw I had entered upon a profession quite congenial to my taste and feelings, and that there was a wide field opened before me for the exercise of that peculiar talent with which I was gifted, although it was wholly out of my power to possess myself of my master's money, as in the case of old Tarrant.

" After I had been a little time in the office of Rap, I put the fruits of my plunder whilst with my former master, into the funds, and by watching the rise and fall of the public securities, I nearly doubled, in the course of four or five years, the original sum I thus had.

When my apprenticeship was served, I had made ample means to take a house in a fashionable street, and furnish it sumptuously. I soon acquired a name for being a most successful and expert solicitor, and business poured in upon me, which was greatly increased by the death of Rap, whose clients all came to me, and amongst the rest Mr. Nipper Norbery, or, as he was usually called, 'Old Hawk,' and his transactions in the bill and bond way were so extensive, that his business was very lucrative, although my engagement with him was to charge him nothing but the costs out of pocket in any suit in which I was not successful, in cases where I succeeded, of course, I made his opponents pay the piper.

" One of the most pleasing circumstances in my whole life occurred to me shortly after I formed my connection with Old Hawk, and it was this : he showed me one day a great number of over-due bills which lay in his drawers for some four or five years. Some of them were paid, and on others balances were due, which he wished to have recovered. Amongst the rest was one endorsed by one of the two country shopkeepers who insisted that I should leave the public vehicle in which they were seated the morning I bid a last adieu to my native town. My heart leaped with joy when I saw it, and having taken it out of the batch, I asked Old Hawk if anything were due on it, and if so, that I would enable him to get the amount, as I had an account of a long standing to settle with one of the endorsers. He looked at his book, and said he could not tell exactly what was due, but he believed there was but a small balance, and some interest. I told him to charge the amount to me, and give me the bill, which he did of course most willingly. Having got it into my possession, I sent down a writ by a trusty bailiff, to be served on the defendent, but the fellow of course knew his business, and having merely visited the house where the man lived, and seen him there, he returned to town, made the usual affidavit of service, upon which the most expensive proceedings were taken, and an execution obtained against the goods of my old travelling companion. I had it held over until I knew the fellow was in Dublin, and then sent to the sheriff, to whom I was in the habit of giving a great deal of business, with instructions to levy the amount with all possible speed before the man could return home and pay the money to save the exposure of a sale.

" My orders were quickly complied with, for by this time I had risen into rank and station ; those who heard of me or knew me in my earlier days seemed to forget everything that related to my past ill fame, and were amongst those who most warmly expressed admiration of my talents and great good fortune ! but I always treated those fellows with the most superlative contempt ; and when some of them would take off their hats to salute me in the streets as I drove by in my chariot, attended by a couple of livery servants, I would scarcely deign to notice them.

" I became a favourite with the aristocracy, and was one of the most admired at soirees, balls, and musical parties, and finally formed, as you know, a matrimonial connection with the daughter of a rich baronet. I had wealth at command, to which I was daily adding by every means that my profession and the law would allow, and as I became reputed for the possession of money, I was in proportion admired as the possessor of every virtue that could adorn the human character.

But I am wandering from the pleasing incident connected with the utter ruin of my old fellow-traveller in the van the morning I set out for Dublin. In a few days after, all his property, amounting to three or four hundred guineas, was sold to pay the bill, (originally thirty-eight pounds) and costs which I had heaped upon it. I saw him one morning coming to my door, pale, dejected, and jaded-looking, he was admitted into the hall, and in the most humble and supplicating tone asked to see the master, he was sent into my study, and on his appearing before me I viewed him with a malicious satisfaction, the very remembrance of which gives me pleasure at this moment, notwithstanding the excruciating pain which I am suffering; he looked abashed, and held down his head, but after recovering a little he began to state the grievances he had suffered at my hands,

when he did not owe a shilling of the debt for which he was sold out. He said he had endorsed the bill to help a friend to raise money from old Norberry, which was paid by instalments, although the document still remained in the hands of the old money-lender, and added, had he been applied to he would have paid it over again sooner than allow his property to be sacrificed in the way it was, and his ruin so completely effected.

"I listened with attention till he had concluded his story, for the recital from his own lips of the misery he had endured gave me additional delight. I then asked

No, 12.

he did remember the morning I left home poor and friendless, when he refused to sit in the same public conveyance with me, and concluded my observations by calling in two servants to put him out. They dragged him to the street door, and pushed him down the steps : he fell on his head, and lay for some minutes weltering in his blood, which flowed from a wound on his face. When he recovered the went to the police office where my friend Councillor Ember presided. This gentleman had recently been appointed to the office he held, and I was in the habit of cashing an old bill for him. I had known him from the time I was serving my apprenticeship, and occassionally gave him half fees on condition of his endorsing the receipt of the whole one on the back of his briefs. Whed he heard the complaint of the poor countryman, he told him he could not believe his statement, but, to keep up an appearance of impartiality and fair play, he sent me a polite message to attend with my two servants to answer the complaint that had been made against me. I attended of course and stated that the complainant had come to my office to offer me insolence, and use threats towards me, for having caused him to pay the amount of his bill, which fell into my hands; that I merely called my servants to remove him as quietly as possible, and that in the struggle he made to resist them he fell down the steps of my hall door, and was hurt. The servants corroborated my story of course, and the worthy magistrate ordered a couple of bailiffs to thrust him out of the office, telling him at the same time, that if he came back again to disturb the court he should be sent to gas for a month. The fellow returned home without any redress, and died in a few months after of the injuries he had received, and, I might add, a broken heart, at the ruin that came so unexpectedly upon him.

"I should have stated, that his fellow-traveller in the van, upon the memorable morning before spoken of, had died some years previously, and was thus unfortunately out of my reach before I had the power to crush him.

"I had many other opportunities, in my professional career, of ruining persons who were obnoxious to me, and thus gratifying that spirit of revenge which was always so dear to my heart; and though I shall not live to glut my vengeance upon that villain Swingsnap, I shall leave after me a memorial which will ultimately lead to his detection, and abstract from him the property he acquired by such infamous means, the heir to which is still living, although I cannot exactly tell where.

"It is unnecessary to enter into a detail of the various transactions I have had with Old Hawk. He was a profitable client, yet I always hated him; for I saw that he understood my real character, and had always been most niggardly in his settlement of costs with me. I therefore felt the greatest satisfaction in having had an opportunity of turning round on him and effecting his ruin.

"But of all the men I ever had to deal with, Swingsnap is the worst. There is much about his manner calculated to deceive. His wit, apparent candour, and frankness of manner, make at once a favourable impression upon all with whom he comes in contact. But he is, in reality, one of the most cruel and bloody-minded of the human race, and is destined to take some prominent part in the ranks of the oppressors of his country, and those whom corruption has arrayed against her. But whyr ecur to his hated name, when it is impossible that I can live to satiate my vengeance on him? I feel that life is fast ebbing sway, and I must hastily conclude this confession.

"I need hardly say that Old Hawk was as sane as any man in existence, and that he commission of lunacy was a dernier resort to dispose of him and keep his property from falling into the hands of the Fogarty family. But I trust Swingsnap shall be ultimately disappointed; for I will leave materials enough behind, |upon which a suit may be hereafter founded, that will not only strip him of the wealth he has thus acquired, but expose his turpitude to the world.

"It has been owing to the nurse of young Norberry that the murder of the child has not been added to the catalogue of his crimes. He made the woman large offers to administer poison to it, but she always refused either to do so or allow it out of her possession, so that the matter was finally arranged by reporting that another child who died from natural causes was the heir to the house of **Norberry**. Wherever that woman now is, she has the child with her.

"He caused, too, the entry of the marriage of Old Hawk to be either erased from the parish book, or the book itself destroyed, so that in case the heir should ever appear, there should be no record to prove his legitimacy.

"In a word, he left nothing undone to secure the possession of his uncle's wealth; but if this coufession be preserved, together with my papers, they will one day lead to his exposure, and the restoration of the property to its lawful heir.

"I have thus unburdened my mind of matter which has been long hidden there, and I have given at least an outline of my own crimes with a candour that ought to insure a ready belief for what I have said regarding others. As to eternity, I have nothing to hope, and nothing to dread. I believe that there shall be an end of me when I breathe my last, and all that is said about a future existence is only iutended to maintain order and make men moral and well-conducted in this world, and if a man be able to keep the appearance of that order and murality, he discharges the duty which society requires, and should be regarded as a good and useful citizen. I have nothing to accuse myself for on that head, for when my mind was intent upon deeds of the blackest eharacter, or had actually accomplished them in secret, I assumed not only the moralily of a true philosopher, but to please the taste of the day, I was in appearance a pious and sincere Christian. I thus acted my part well and would have run on a glorious career but that it has been cut short by this fatal duel with Swingsnap."

The wretched Gripe here ceased his narrative. His dissolution was evidently at hand; his face became livid, a yellow froth covered his lips; he became delirious, attempted to do violence to those about him, and when tied down in the bed, he roared and foamed like a person affected with hydrophobia, and at the end of one of those paroxysms, which continued for a day and a night, he breathed his last. It was found that the wounded part had become putrified, and full of large maggots, and such was the horrible effluvia emitted from his dead body, that it was with difficulty the undertakers could place it in a coffin. It was removed a few hours after life became extinct, and interred at night in the church of ———, where a handsome marble monument has been erected to his memory, which gives the lie direct to his own dying confession.

Wormwood now became the confidential solicitor of Swingsnap, and expressed his deep delight at having his revenge against his old professional opponent so soon and so fnlly gratified.

Gripe was soon forgotten by all, except those who had been made the victim of his depravity and deceit. There were, to be sure, some vague rumours afloa with regard to the confession he had made implicating Swingsnap; but they, too, were forgotten, in proportion to the rapid advances in the world that were made by the young barrister, whose wealth and audacity soon gave him great influence. He abused all who were opposed to him in unmeasured terms of scurrility, and in a few months after the death of Gripe, he received a hostile message from the leading counsel opposed to him in a cause in the Exchequer, in which he had a brief from his friend Wormwood. He was punctual to the call made upon him to give satisfaction, and at five in the morning he and his old second, and one or two friends, were seen upon the beach at Sandymount, waiting for the opposite party, who did not come, and it was only when leaving the ground, after shivering there for an hour on a frosty morning, that an account twas brought to him that his opponent had been seized with a fit of gout during the night, and of course was unable to attend. This was a fresh triumph, but a till more profitable one as regarded his professional career.

The cause out of which the dispute arose had been adjourned

that morning, and he and Wormwood hastened into town, were in the Exchequer when the court sat, ready to proceed with the cause, while there was no appearance on the part of counsel on the opposite side. The rumour of the duel had spread through town the previous evening, and when Swingsnap was found in court urging on his case, and his opponent absent, there was a rush by all the "hall men" to get in to have a peep at him, and there he was impressing on their lordships the necessity of proceeding in the matter, as further delay would be the ruin of his client. The absence of counsel, who did not think proper to ask for a postponement, or send any explanation to the court with regard to his non-attendance, was not deserving of indulgence, and he trusted their lordships would, for the sake of precedent, allow him to proceed.

"He shot his man," whispered some of the gentlemen in the bar [seats, "and after doing his work he is here as unconcerned as if nothing had happened,"

Some conjectured, with more truth, that perhaps he frightened the life out of him, whilst the curiosity of all was stretched to the utmost to know what was the fate of the poor councillor.

The cause went on, and was decided in favour of the client of Swingsnap, although in stating it he manifested great ignorance of the principles of law, but his assurance and perseverance carried him through every difficulty.

Duels at that time between members of the bar and of the Irish house were looked upon as ordinary occurrences of the day, and the man who had the real courage to not accept an invitation to be shot at could not hold up his head in society, but he who actually sent a hostile message, and then, as the report ran, was seized with cramps, from terror of the prospect before him, dare hardly show his face, and was shunned like a plague; so that Swingsnap's challenger, although a man then of considerable business, was, poor fellow, completely snuffed out; and the government of the day, with whom he had some interest, were obliged to provide for him by giving an appointment in the colonies.

Wormwood and Swingsnap had now to turn their attention to the best means of recovering the bags of gold that had been taken possession of by Gripe on the day that unfortunate Old Hawk was dragged off to the mad-house, but in this, as might be anticipated, they had some obstacles to contend with.

Wormwood, however, took the necessary proceedings, and after considerable delays and difficulties, he, through the integrity of Gripe's apprentice, who counted over the money before his master's death, recovered it back for his client, minus the costs and funeral expenses, which should fairly be deducted from it.

Swingsnap had now a clear road opened before him, and nothing to obstruct him; and whilst himself and his new solicitor are congratulating themselves upon their success, the reader must return to the cell of poor blind Tim in the lunatic side of Newgate, to which he had been considerately consigned by the care of the Mountrath-street magistrates, and the agency of Gripe and his client.

From the moment of his committal he appeared to exhibit the most pious resignation to his fate, and if anything at times disturbed his repose, it was his anxious solicitude to know what had become of his old master. When the intelligence of his death reached him, he seemed to think that there was no hope for him on this side of the grave, and, in a few months afterwards he died, attended by a minister of his religion, and with the most perfect assurance of a happy eternity. His friends had his remains interred in the little churchyard on the right-hand side of the road between Rockbrook and the mountain of Killikee, some three or four miles beyond Rathfarnham, and it may be truly said, that the grave never closed over the remains of a more virtuous, simple-hearted, faithful, and affectionate servant. In several years after his death, the extraordinary incidents connected with himself and his master reached the ears of the late Mrs. Oakley, of Oakley House, near whose demesne the little churchyard is situated, and she caused a handsome stone to be cut, and placed over his grave, on which is the following inscription:—"This monument was erected by Mrs. Oakley, to mark the spot which contains the ashes of Timothy M'Dermott, whose fidelity and affection to his master, the late ——, deserve to be commemorated."

Many who have heard the incidents connected with the fate of poor Tim and his master, have often paid a visit to his grave, sighed for the sorrows he had suffered, and prayed that his merits and his virtues might meet their reward in another world.

CHAPTER IX.

A LONG HIATUS IN THE FAMILY MEMOIRS.—DISCOVERY OF THE SON OF KATE.—CONCLUSION.

YEARS rolled on after the death of Old Hawk and the other principal actors in the tragic scenes which the first part of these memoirs present to the reader. Nothing was heard of the heir, whom the confession of Gripe represented as being still in existence : and those who remembered anything of the disasters of the Fogarty family, and the miserable end of old Norberry, believed that the story of Gripe, which, at the time of his death, had been generally circulated, was not founded on fact, and that Swingsnap, or Swing, as he was commonly called, was in the enjoyment of wealth legitimately his own ; that his old uncle had, in point of fact, died mad : and this supposition was strengthened by some traditionary tales of a madman of that name, who figured in the time of Cromwell, and who was the ancestor of the Norberry family. The fate of the Fogartys was forgotten by all but the amiable Mrs. Cavanagh and her family, who, for many years, were in the habit of going on Sundays to their grave, in the Hospital Fields, there to breathe a sigh and shed a tear at this remembrance of their unmerited sorrows, and offer up a prayer that they might enjoy felicity in a happy and eternal home, far beyond the reach of tyranny, oppression, and deceit.

In the meantime, Swingsnap was most successful in his practice at the bar, not by talent and application to his profession, but by ready wit, bullying, and downright assurance. He was married to the daughter of Wormwood, with whom he got a large fortune, which, added to the property acquired by the death of his uncle, made him one of the most wealthy men at the Irish bar. He was a reputed " fireeater," and got a good deal of business from clients, under the impression that the counsel opposed to him were afraid that, when foiled in law or argument, he would offer them some insult, that would make it imperative on them to meet him in deadly combat. He was, besides, taken great notice of by the government, who were in want of daring and audacious men to assist them in carrying their measures through parliament, in which he obtained a seat, having been first made attorney-general. All who knew him wondered at his good fortune, and those who envied and hated him were afraid to give utterance to their opinions.

It is always a most promising incident in the beginning of the career of an aspiring public man to kill his antagonist in a duel. Gripe. though a coward, was accounted one of the best pistol-shots then in Dublin : and the man who not only had the courage to meet him, but the unerring aim to shoot him, was looked upon as a perfect Achilles. Besides, he had always expressed the utmost disregard for life, and on one occasion accepted the challenge of a master tailor with whom he had a dispute about a suit of clothes, but when poor Snip went to the ground, he became sick, and was unable to fight.

Swingsnap was, therefore, dreaded by many of the bar, and was often allowed to bully and abuse his antagonists with impunity. The Irish people, who always admire a man of prowess and courage, brought him their business until he got beyond their reach, by having been made attorney-general. Whilst he held that office, he added much to his already great wealth, for he directed and conducted more prosecutions at the suit of the crown, within three or four years, than any of his predecessors had done in treble the time. We shall leave him, thus pursuing a prosperous career, whilst we turn to another part of the globe, where the reader will meet with an old acquaintance.

Amongst a batch of recruits sent out from England to the East Indies, in the year 18——, was a lad named Robert Norberry, of delicate and very prepossessing appearance, who, during the voyage, won the esteem and excited the curiosity of the officer who had charge of the party. They landed safe at Bombay, and proceeded up the country to Bangalore, where the —— regiment was stationed, of which the reader's old friend, O'Kelly, by that time a veteran in the service, was major. The morning after their arrival, and when upon drill, the gallant officer walked up the ranks to inspect the European recruits that had been sent out to him, and when he came to Robert, he stopped and exclaimed, " This young man's face has a strong resemblance to one deeply fixed in my memory : his appearance has in an instant called up within my mind the recollection of events, which now seem to me like a troubled dream long past. My lad, what is your name ? from whence do you come ? "

" My name is Robert," said the young recruit ; " I believe Robert Norberry, but of that I am not sure : I had friends of the name of Walpole in the county of Wicklow, in Ireland, who are dead : I had been called after them for some time, but I have reason to believe that they were not related to me in the most remote degree, and that my name is Norberry."

" This is mysterious," said O'Kelly ; " your history must be minutely inquired into ;" and as he spoke, he gazed with earnestness on the outlines of as handsome a face as could belong to a youth of twenty-one. " Norberry! Norberry! you are the son of my first love—of Kate Fogarty. · If I am right in my conjecture, there is more than chance in our meeting under such peculiar circumstances in this remote quarter of the globe. The finger of Providence is manifest in this extaordinary event. My heart swells with indiscribable emotions, as it whispers to me that this is the son of her whom I once loved to distraction, who was sacrificed by her parents in the hope of obtaining wealth, and whose melancholy fate ought to be a warning to all who would rend asunder the tenderest of all human ties, and violate feelings consecrated by Heaven, in the hopes of earthly gain. The sad story of Kate Fogarty contains a moral by which all should profit who hear it, and I trust that some faithful chronicler shall yet give it to the world."

O'Kelly listened with great attention to the story of Norberry's adventures, and day by day became more attached to the young man. The worthy major had a daughter, a charming girl of seventeen, who shared all her father's sympathy for Norberry's misfortunes ; sympathy ripened into love, and in due time they married, and the whole family returned to Ireland. It is not our intention to relate their good and bad fortunes at length ; suffice it to say that ineffectual attempts were made to wrest the Norberry property from Chief Justice Swingsnap, and that the expenses consequent on the suit exhausted the savings of O'Kelly, who died eventually in obscurity, and was soon followed by his daughter and unfortunate son-in-law ; and thus concludes our tale of successful villany and disappointed affection.

THE END.

London: Printed and Published by E. Lloyd, 12, Salisbury-square, Fleet-street.

www.ingramcontent.com/pod-product-compliance
Lightning Source LLC
Chambersburg PA
CBHW081211170626
46811CB00010B/3249